SHIP'S ANGEL

D1628145

Also by Bridget Crowley:

Step into the Dark
Feast of Fools

SHIP'S ANGEL

BRIDGET CROWLEY

Hodder
Children's
Books

A division of Hodder Headline Limited

Copyright © 2004 Bridget Crowley

First published in Great Britain in 2004
by Hodder Children's Books

The right of Bridget Crowley to be identified as the author
of this work has been asserted by her in accordance with the
Copyright, Designs and Patents Act 1988.

10 9 8 7 6 5 4 3 2 1

All rights reserved. Apart from any use permitted under
UK copyright law, this publication may only be reproduced,
stored or transmitted, in any form, or by any means with
prior permission in writing of the publishers or in the case of
reprographic production in accordance with the terms of
licences issued by the Copyright Licensing Agency and may
not be otherwise circulated in any form of binding or cover
other than that in which it is published and without a similar
condition being imposed on the subsequent purchaser.

All characters in this publication are fictitious and any
resemblance to real persons, living or dead,
is purely coincidental.

A Catalogue record for this book is available
from the British Library

ISBN 0 340 88155 0

Typeset in Palatino by Avon DataSet Ltd,
Bidford-on-Avon, Warwickshire

Printed and bound in Great Britain by
Clays Ltd, St Ives plc

The paper and board used in this paperback by
Hodder Children's Books are natural recyclable products
made from wood grown in sustainable forests.
The manufacturing processes conform to the environmental
regulations of the country of origin.

Hodder Children's Books
A division of Hodder Headline Limited
338 Euston Road
London NW1 3BH

To Jon A, John's midwife,
with thanks and much affection

MORAY COUNCIL LIBRARIES & INFO.SERVICES	
2O 14 O1 15	
Askews	
JCY	

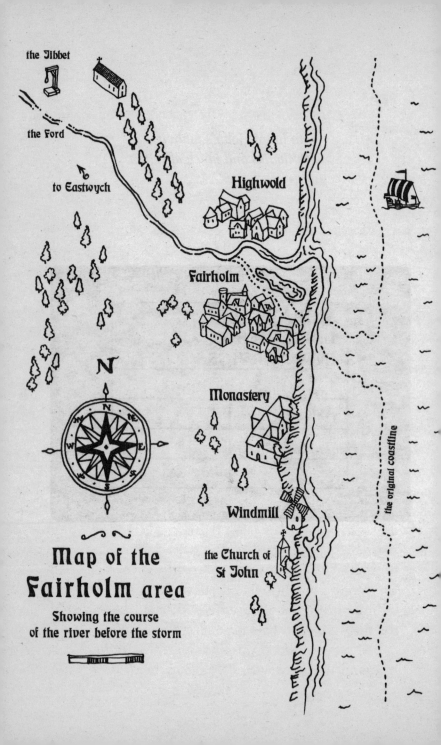

the Jibbet

the Ford

to Eastwych

Highwold

Fairholm

N

Monastery

Windmill

the Church of
St John

the original coastline

Map of the
Fairholm area

Showing the course
of the river before the storm

Chapter 1

The look-out screamed against the wind, his hair streaming out behind him, his tunic flapping, wrapping tightly round bare legs blue with cold.

' 'Tis the *Elephant*, sir. Comin' up on us fast!'

John glanced up at the top-castle clinging like a bird's nest high, high up on the mast, lurching in the heavy swell. The look-out was straining to look astern through the flying spray, waving his arms frantically and pointing into the distance. John wiped his eyes and peered out across the heaving sea. Another ship, a cog, much larger than their little hulk the *Esperance*, was speeding through the white foam curling up round its prow, faster and faster, gaining on them, there was no doubt. He looked around him at the crew. They were worried. They muttered, crossed themselves, peered astern, hurried about their business, sure-footed on the wet boards and high above on the yard. John shifted uneasily, still unused to the giddy feeling of walking on water and telling his stomach to be quiet. What was this ship, the *Elephant*, that was following them? Why?

The crew climbed nimbly about the rigging, bare legs and feet raw with cold. They heaved on ropes with calloused hands. John heaved with them on sheet or shroud – or whatever the ropes were called – he would fumble, making a mess of coiling or furling, splashing about trying to row, and they would grin at his efforts or cheer him on. But now they moved around him deftly, tense and intent, trying to make the little hulk fly faster across the heaving backs of the waves, while he kept out of the way, damp, unsteady and bewildered, limping on his damaged foot and wishing himself anywhere but here.

Why was the *Elephant* chasing them?

The Master stood up on the raised stern-castle behind him. Grim-faced and spattered with spray, he seemed to be urging their own ship forward, shoulders hunched, leaning with the wind, bellowing the occasional order at the men scurrying round him.

'They got a second sail, blast their eyes!'

Two gnarled, red-faced crewmen paused close to John, now below him, now above as the deck reared up beneath them like a great animal humping its back. First he could see the scudding clouds, then a bottomless pit of swirling water.

'Christ Jesu save us, then,' said the second man. 'Two sails! I 'eard tell of new ships with two sails, but I never seen 'em. They'll 'ave us now.'

John peered back through a mist of spray at the *Elephant* bearing down behind them, so much bigger than the *Esperance*. He ran a hand over his wet face. They had a second mast, shorter and a little in front of the main mast. On it, a strange triangular sail was jerking upwards, bellying out in the wind as it rose. The *Elephant* seemed to leap forward even faster.

The Master roared and the mate pulled on the great rudder over the side of the ship. The men hurled themselves into action and someone shoved a rope into John's hand.

'Pull, for Jesu's sake. Pull, boy . . .'

John pulled; his foot slid on the slippery boards, but he jammed it under a heavy rope and hung on, heaving with all his might. At last here was something he could do. As they pulled in unison, the mate called out a rhythm. They echoed it with a loud grunt on each tug, gathering strength between each effort. Slowly the heavy yard above them swung round and the hulk veered round with it, keeling over further and further, till a sudden huge wave burst over the side, taking John unawares. He staggered under the weight of the water, spluttering and spitting, wet through and shivering. But still the *Elephant* came on behind them, closer and closer.

'Arm yourselves!'

The Master drew a sword. The men scattered, pulling out knives, picking up lengths of rope, tugging bits of wood or crowbars from under the tarpaulin where part of the cargo was stacked on the foredeck. They turned to face the oncoming ship. John had nothing he could use as a weapon, but suddenly he remembered his father's tool bag, hidden under the tarpaulin. He dragged out a viciously pointed chisel. What would his father have said, using his beautiful tool as a weapon . . . but he had to do something. The men around him seemed desperate. One of the crew threw him a grin and he tried a grin back. The others were already setting up catcalls of defiance.

The cog was nearly upon them, men massed on the forecastle, towering above them, brandishing missiles, yelling abuse. 'Get over there, boy,' yelled Hairy Jack, the sailor who had grinned. He jerked his head at the tarpaulin. 'Get underneath.' But John gripped his chisel and stood his ground. The man gave a brief nod and they pressed together with the others, nine or ten men against two dozen or more on the bigger ship.

Rocks and stones rained down around them from the top-castle of the *Elephant*. A heavy boulder smashed a great tear in the ship's side and a sheet of water shot through. An iron bar shot past John's ear and punched a hole in the decking at his feet. He leapt back and went flying, sliding across the deck, grabbing at anything he could to stop himself. Hairy Jack yanked him to his feet. He shook himself and took a breath.

The cog lay alongside now. Reddened hands with nails hardened into claws reached over and grasped the gunwale, heaving the two ships closer together. The men of the *Esperance* beat and kicked at them, trying to fend them off, but a ladder was slung over and a couple of ropes and inexorably the crew of the *Elephant* began to swarm across, carrying knives, swords and cudgels. They were met by a fury of blows but on they came, some hacking at the rigging, the ropes suddenly flying free in the wind and lashing at faces. John laid about him with the chisel. He heard a cry as, almost by accident, he ripped open the arm of an enemy sailor. He stopped, his mouth open in horror. He felt the Master's hand clap him on the back.

'Well done, lad, that's it. Go to. On.'

The Master was beside them, fighting alongside, but John still froze, looking down at the blood on his chisel. A blow at the side of his head sent him spinning. He landed against the tarpaulin and scrabbled up on top of the heap of cargo. Below him on the deck, the mate was on his back, struggling under the weight of a huge sailor from the cog. John launched himself and fastened his arms round his neck, tightening his grip till the man rolled over, scratching and tugging at John's arms. The mate sprang to his feet, landed a punch in the sailor's belly and finished him off with a blow to his chin. John dropped off on to the deck, winded.

'Ye'll do, lad,' said the mate, and disappeared into the fray.

A thud behind John signalled another enemy sailor landing on the deck. He whipped round. The man was tall and wiry and high above his head he held a flaming torch guttering in the wind. He shoved John aside and wriggled between the heaving bodies towards the sail. John yelled at the Master but his voice was lost in the din of brawling bodies, the wind and the waves. The mate was already entangled with another sailor.

His eyes on the torch, John squeezed through the furious fighting after him. The man reached up, balancing with one foot on the gunwale, and held the torch to the sail. But the sail was wet. It scorched a little but the flame wouldn't take hold. The man stretched further along the boom, still holding the torch against it, swearing and muttering as he went. John followed. There was no way he could tackle the man straight on, or even from the back. He would be overboard before he could blink. The man reached up further. John took a breath. Closing his eyes, he stabbed his chisel hard into the bare calf above him and turned it, driving the tool further into the man's muscle. The sailor shrieked and fell, dropping the torch.

Without stopping to think, John snatched it up and clambered back on to the cargo. Stumbling over a couple of writhing bodies, he flung the torch as hard as he could overboard. He turned away, not noticing the wind spin it, still flaring, up and over. It landed on the *Elephant*, and lay sputtering on some barrels on the deck. John dropped down exhausted, wiping his chisel on the tarpaulin, sickened by the thought of it sticking into the sailor's flesh. How ... how could he have done it? Surely the chisel his father had once used to carve all those beautiful angels in the cathedral could never seem the same. He sat, miserable and sick, his wet clothes clinging to him and weighing him down.

Suddenly there was a cry. Men were crowding to the side of the little ship, the men of the *Esperance* cheering, the enemy sailors bellowing in fury. The *Elephant* was on fire. Together, her crew leapt back across to their ship, but three of them fell with a shriek between the two vessels and disappeared into the turbulent grey waves. John scrambled to his knees. What had happened? He watched the blaze and suddenly realized that somehow it must have been the torch he had thrown that had landed over there and set the ship alight. He shook his head in disbelief.

' 'Tis their oil barrels,' yelled a sailor with a great laugh. 'They're afire.'

Over on the *Elephant*, the panicking crew were flailing about with bits of tarpaulin, heaving buckets from the sea to put out the fire. With a roar, the strange shape of the foresail, raised only moments before the attack, suddenly went up in a sheet of flame. There had been no time for it to become wet and it burned merrily against the grey sky.

'That'll teach 'em to use that newfangled nonsensical stuff,' said the mate, hawking and spitting. Then he called the men back to order. John clambered to his feet.

'We must put in ashore.' The Master called the mate to him and spoke in a low voice. 'This is not what I planned nor what I would wish, but she won't reach Flanders with a hole in her side and the rigging like it is. We need repairs. Fairholm harbour is close and I've a friend there who'll help. I'll need to borrow money.' He looked worried as he climbed back up to the stern-castle and called out an order. Not for the first time, John noticed that the Master favoured one foot, limping sometimes almost as much as he did himself.

For a moment the sail flapped uselessly, but willing hands caught at flying ropes and struggled to control it. Behind them, the *Elephant* drifted helplessly. The fire on board was dying, but an occasional leaping flame tipped the grey waves with brilliant orange and a shower of fiery stars shot into the air. The *Esperance* yawed and turned towards a thin dark grey line above the sea on the horizon. John looked up at the Master, then back to the distant shore, not unhappy at the thought of dry land. At least his stomach might behave itself there.

He settled down on the tarpaulin and dragged out his tools, wiping his chisel again and again to make sure no blood remained on the blade. When it was clean he took out the piece of stone he had been carving since he had arrived in Kingsbridge, the port from which they had set sail and where the Master had found him, cold and half-starved on the wharf.

Perhaps it was the sight of John's limp, so like his own, that made him take pity on him and listen to his story, the story of how the scaffolding in the cathedral had fallen, taken his father's life and injured his own foot all in one blow. He heard the story of the death of his friend Hugh and the terrible man who had killed him. He heard of the disappearance of Aaron and the other Jews who had been blamed for all the ills of the great city in which they had lived. No one had been able to say where the Jews had gone, they had vanished. But the Master seemed to think they might have gone to Flanders, a place that he knew well and where his ship was going with a cargo of fleeces for the weavers there. He had offered to carry John with him. He would have to work his passage as best he could, ignorant as he was of ships and the sea. And John, with nothing to lose, nothing to stay for, had decided to go. The thought of Aaron, and of the tall, kindly, dignified man who was Aaron's father, seemed to beckon him from the depths of his misery.

He chipped away at the tiny stone angel, careful to set up a kind of rhythm that fitted with the rise and fall of the ship. Hairy Jack squatted beside him.

'Well, young Peg-leg . . .'

Jack looked up, ready to be angry if it was an insult, but oddly comforted at the sound of the name he had been labelled with at the choir school in the city. Hairy Jack grinned.

'You done all right, young 'un,' he said. John tilted his head on one side as a question. 'Back there.' The brawny sailor jerked his head towards the cog, still burning away further and further behind them. 'You ain't much of a sailor now, that's true, but you done all right in a fight.'

John shrugged, ashamed of what he had done with the chisel that was now about its rightful business under his hand. He ran his palm over the stone, feeling its cool contours, curves and ridges, brushing off the stone dust that gathered in crevices.

'What's that you got there?'

'It's – it's an angel. Like one my father made once . . .' His voice died away and he swallowed.

'Your father a stonemason?'

John nodded, curtly.

'No wonder you ain't much of a sailor then, eh?' Hairy Jack laughed and slapped John's knee with a huge hand sprouting black hairs all over the back. 'Where is 'e now?'

John swallowed again and sighed, chewing his lip. 'Dead?'

John nodded. 'There was an accident. The scaffolding fell in the cathedral, just when . . . just when he was putting up the last angel.'

'So that's why you made that little feller.' Hairy Jack nodded at the angel in John's hand. John didn't answer. 'My father drowned at sea when I were your age. Didn't stop me going for a sailor. I guess I were one already . . .' The man shrugged. 'Guess you'll go for a stonemason just the same too.'

It was John's turn to shrug.

'Why you 'ere, then? Why ain't ye back there at that cathedral?'

Suddenly, John felt too tired to explain.

'I'm . . . I'm looking for someone,' he said.

Hairy Jack stood up, stretched and scratched his chest. Thick hairs sprouted through his sacking shirt. Thick black curls tumbled under his seaman's bonnet, tied tight under his chin to keep the hair out of his eyes in the wind.

' 'Ope you find 'em,' he said, with an eye at the mate who was beginning to lay about him with a whip, cracking it not at anyone in particular, but round about a few men lying exhausted on the deck. 'Landfall in a couple of hours,' he said and started up the rigging with the other sailors, high up on to the yard. John stood up. He looked at the Master, ready to climb with them, but the Master shook his head and John tried not to feel relieved.

He looked towards the shore. Nearer now, with a few buildings discernible: a windmill, a church tower, a few masts like blackened skeletons behind a long sandbank covered in tough, wiry grass. Grey grass, knotted and windswept, not like the soft green grass of the hills he had left behind.

He glanced up at the Master leaning on the parapet of the stern-castle, quite still, gazing towards the shore. Quietly, he spoke to the mate, in a voice too low for John to hear. The mate handed the rudder to a sailor and leapt up beside the Master. Together they stared this way and that, searching for something, frowning, puzzled, and then seeming almost afraid. The other sailors paused at their work, all of them looking towards the land.

'What has God sent to us now?' John heard the Master say. 'What has happened? Where is it? Fairholm should be forward as we go. It's a great port. We can't have missed it, for Jesu's sake. And that's the windmill, and the tower is the church of St John. I'd recognize them anywhere.'

The mate crossed himself.

'Saint Nicholas guide us, it's the devil's work,' he said. 'Where's the rest of the town ... and the harbour entrance?'

Silently, the crew seemed to draw together and look at the Master to tell them what to do, what was happening. They whispered amongst themselves and he looked at them angrily.

'I know no more than you,' he said. 'We'll put in and find out. There must be some explanation.'

'Maybe 'e's got us lost,' muttered a sailor, glancing up at the Master and looking away quickly in case he was overheard.

'Not the Master,' said Hairy Jack. ' 'E knows this coast. And so do I. Something ain't right over there,' and he nodded towards the shore, his brows furrowed and his eyes anxious.

'Devil's work,' said the sailor and crossed himself. 'You see if it ain't.'

'Never mind the devil's work, get about yer own.' The mate cracked his whip again. Hushed and mutinous, the men went about their business, some with their wounds from the battle with the *Elephant* bound up with filthy old bits of sailcloth, others with great bruises already turning purple and swelling up. They were all still there, no one had been lost, but now they faced a different fear. Had a whole town disappeared? Had the devil stopped up the harbour mouth?

John stood, his angel in his hand, and gazed at the fast-approaching coastline. There was no break in the sandbank that he could see, no welcoming port, no way in at all, just spiky grey grass and beyond it a few stunted trees with silver leaves, shivering in the wind. The windmill sails were still and one hung loose. It was as if the harbour had never existed.

Chapter 2

The *Esperance* scoured the coast from a distance for an hour or more. The Master himself took a turn to labour on the great rudder, the mate's whip flicking the air, the men grumbling and swearing as they hauled on ropes to heave her round, back and forth, back and forth. Twice the look-out yelled a sighting that turned out to be nothing. Nearer and nearer the long unbroken line of the pebbles she came, till they could hear the surf surging over them, pounding against the red sandstone cliffs just beyond them away to the left. Larboard, starboard? John could never remember which was which. He hauled with the men as best he could, still wet; but at least the endless pulling kept him warm. Next to him, Hairy Jack muttered with the rest.

' 'Tis gone. It ain't there no more. What's wrong with 'em? Why keep on looking when there ain't no harbour mouth, nowhere? I dunno.'

A man keeled over and lay on the deck. Water slopped over the sides of the ship, swirled round him and ran out through the bilges again as she listed in the swell. Hairy Jack went to help him, but the whip licked round his ankles and he snatched up the

13

rope again, hissing through his teeth and looking murder at the mate. The man lying on the deck had a terrible wound on his arm, his face pale as death as the water swilled round him. His eyes were closed.

'We're making water,' said the mate. He shoved a leather bucket at John and yanked up a couple of boards in the decking. 'Get below and bail.'

John dropped down on to the cargo, almost toppling and pitching further into the black hole. He steadied himself and stooped to balance among the bales of wool fleeces. Gingerly, he felt around beneath him. The bales were dry at the top but soaking beneath. He lowered the bucket into the darkness. It gurgled and filled with evil-smelling water that he slewed out across the deck above his head, once, twice, then on and on, till his back ached and his shoulders felt they would come out of their sockets.

Suddenly, he heard the look-out cry out again far above, this time it seemed with real hope in his voice. John stopped bailing and peered out, his head poking from the hole in the deck. The look-out was jabbing the air with an excited arm, pointing way down the coast to a darker line in the sandbank. The whip whistled past John's ear and he set to again, quickly. Overhead, he heard the thud of the Master's limping stride as he hurried to the side of the ship.

'I see it.' John heard him overhead, muttering almost to himself. 'Not where it should be, but it's there. And that's St John's church at Fairholm, I'm certain. Well . . . in she goes.'

The *Esperance* seemed to put on a spurt as if eager to make safe harbour, and the men took heart, even cheering under their breath. John's hands were sore and his shoulders aching, but he looked up with a grin through the hole at Hairy Jack above him. But the big sailor wasn't smiling. He shook his head and his black curls bobbed about on his red cheeks under his seaman's bonnet.

'Don't like it,' he said, quietly. 'We asked the blessed Saint Nicholas, but he ain't with us this time.'

'Saint Nicholas?' said John, remembering the plays of Saint Nicholas they had practised at the choir school.

'Our saint. Listens to the prayers of seamen, special, like. Didn't ye know that?'

John shook his head. Saint Nicholas must be busy. He was the children's saint, he knew, but sailors too?

'But if we're going into the harbour, we won't need him, will we?' he said. 'That's good, isn't it? It'll be good to be on land and get repaired?'

'Stow yer garbage, lad.' Hairy Jack glanced about him anxiously. 'Wait till we get there,' he said, his voice almost inaudible under the creaking of the ship.

Puzzled, John bent to his bailing, but for a while the bucket had been getting less and less full till there was only a trickle in the bottom. He stopped, resting his chin on his arms. As the *Esperance* rolled forward over a wave, dipping her nose, he looked up and saw that they were much closer in now. The cliffs were behind them, lost in a thin mist that lay in silvery strands over the sea, shifting in a wind that had dropped to a stiff breeze. Ahead the fog was patchy but thicker. The pebbles gave way to huge sand dunes that loomed towards them. Beyond them

15

he caught the occasional glimpse of another stretch of water like a long, narrow inland sea and beyond that pebbles again, rising steeply to scrubby grass that seemed to stretch on for ever to be lost in the fog.

John heaved himself up from the hold, rammed the planks back into place and dumped the bucket on deck, tying it to a ring in the mast. When he stood upright the men were craning forward, watching intently as a small boat seemed to materialize through the mist out of the sandbanks themselves. John could see four men straining at the oars, smoothly dipping, pulling, dipping, pulling. The little craft sped along. It vanished into a patch of mist then reappeared. The Master called an order and the crew of the *Esperance* raced up into the rigging. Within seconds the big square sail, a brown scorch mark along the base, was furled and tied down neatly to the boom. In silence, the men hung on in the rigging, watching the little boat approach. The Master waved a greeting and a voice carried out to them.

'You're for Highwold?'

'Fairholm!'

A laugh echoed across the water. The Master drew back.

'Nothing left of Fairholm. 'Tis Highwold or nothing, my friend.'

The Master turned to the mate, his face anxious. Hairy Jack dropped down on to the deck.

'I knew it,' he said to John. 'There's trouble. There's been a storm, a cliff fall, something. This coast's treacherous. And I don't just mean the land, neither.'

He stared out at the small boat almost alongside them, his arms across his chest, thoughtfully scratching one hairy armpit.

'I'll wager there ain't no harbour left at Fairholm and they're Highwold men.'

'What does that mean?'

'It do mean out of the cooking pot into the fire,' said a red-haired young sailor. He sucked in his lower lip and bit it with big teeth.

'There ain't no love lost between Highwold and Fairholm men,' said Jack, shaking his head. 'And the Master is a Fairholm man. Not born and bred, mind, but he's known there. Folk there think of 'im as one of 'em. That's where we was going to get help, but now . . .'

'We won't get into Fairholm nor any other harbour without money . . .' said the red-haired sailor.

'If Fairholm's still there . . .'

'It'll still be there,' said the redhead, 'smaller than it was, but it can't 'ave vanished off the face of the earth.' He glanced back at the church tower behind them on the clifftop.

'Nay. It'll just be the way in that's gone,' he said, 'sanded up I'd wager. The cliffs back there didn't seem to 'ave taken much of a tumble. But there was piles of rocks further back down the coast a bit, nearer St John's.'

'You're right, young Lou, it looks like Highwold or nothing. It'll cost the Master a mint and this bunch comin' up on us now is the only way we'll get there.' He jerked a thumb at the little boat almost on them, the men shipping their oars ready to board.

'Can't we sail in?' said John.

The redhead gave him a pitying look.

'Ye don't know nothing, do ye, poor innocent.' Then he shook his head fiercely, spat, and turned away from the sight of a man from the small boat climbing up the rope-ladder the mate had tossed down the side of the ship.

John's spirits sank. Were there always to be fighting and arguments between people? He had thought the cathedral, with its quarrelling canons and money-grubbing hangers-on, left far behind. Where were the people like his father, honest and happy to do the work they loved without wrangling and dispute? Why had they been attacked? Why did they have to face going ashore in fear?

He watched the man from the boat, the Master and the mate, all at loggerheads, banging the air with fists, turning away then back again. Finally, the Master shrugging his shoulders, seeming reluctant, they struck hands in a bargain. The man hurried down the ladder, taking two of the *Esperance* crew with him. Ropes went flying over the gunwales and slithered down to the crew below. They tied them to the little boat heaving gently in the swell and took up their oars, six men now to pull the heavy weight of the hulk across to the river-mouth. The *Esperance*, no longer a proud sailing ship, was under tow. She was going to safe harbour perhaps, but at the mercy of these strangers who had, no doubt, exacted a fine fat fee for the privilege of their protection.

Hastily, John lifted the tarpaulin to see that his tools were still safe. He felt the shape of the little stone angel and pressed it hard, feeling its rough shape through the leather. Surely, it couldn't be stupid to hope, not while there were things to be done like – like making angels. Pulling the tarpaulin back over the bag, he turned to Hairy Jack and the red-haired sailor, who were squatting down on the cargo not far away. He limped across to them.

'Well then, young Peg-leg,' said Hairy Jack.

'Just Peg'll do.'

Lou grinned. 'Short and sweet, eh? Like me. I'm Louis. But Lou's better.'

'Loowee?' Hairy Jack raised a bushy eyebrow. 'I never knew that. You never said. What kind o' name's that?'

Lou lowered his voice and glanced round. 'Me da was French stock, but . . .'

Hairy Jack drew back. 'Fre-ench?' His voice shot up an octave.

Lou grinned and gave him a shove. 'That don't mean I'm in league with the devil. I just don't let it get about too much, not round these parts anyway.'

'Best not,' said Hairy Jack emphatically.

John sat down beside them. Beneath them the *Esperance* laboured on, responding to every tiny wave and every pull of the oars.

'You'll be glad to get ashore,' said Lou. John nodded without enthusiasm. 'No?'

'Well, yes,' said John, 'I will, but . . .'

'Ye don't sound too sure. Ye ain't no sailor, that's for sure,' said Lou. He laughed but not unkindly.

'No,' said John apologetically, 'I don't understand it all, all those different names for things, shrouds and sheets and halyards and that. Why not just call them ropes? That's what they are, isn't it?'

'Stow yer garbage, Peg,' said Hairy Jack with a grin. 'Any road, ye done all right in the fight.'

John shrugged. He could not help but be pleased at Jack's approval, but wished it were for a better reason. He couldn't be proud of what he'd done. He shifted uneasily at the memory of that fat calf above him, the chisel sticking into it and the blood flowing.

'Well,' said Lou, 'it's as well ye can take care of yourself. You may need it where we're goin',' and he nodded towards the shore. 'Still,' he said, giving Hairy Jack a nudge in the ribs, 'we'll get a quart or two down us while we're there I'll wager. Not so bad, eh?'

The two vessels were nearing the shore. John held his breath. The river-mouth looked too narrow to take the hulk but the Master held the rudder and she slipped neatly into the narrow inlet between high sandbanks. For a moment it looked as if they would hit another bank in front of them head-on, but the ship veered just in time and continued on up the meandering river-mouth through patches of mist.

The light was fading rapidly. John and the two sailors climbed up on to the tarpaulin for a better view, holding on to the shrouds to peer out at the passing landscape. At first there was nothing but sand, pebbles and rough grass, then a few trees and suddenly, black and decaying, the ribs of an old rowing-boat sticking up from a patch of mud. A single black bird perched motionless on one of the ragged ends of wood, its long neck curved back, its beak skywards, holding out its wings to dry like crooked arms. Lou crossed himself quickly and looked away.

'What's wrong?' said John.

'That great black bird,' said Lou. ' 'Tis a cormorant. They do say they're the devil wearin' feathers. Bode evil, they do.' John looked back at the bird. It preened its wings and settled, staring over the water with glittering topaz eyes. He shivered.

The mist began to thicken again but to his right, perched on a rise set back a little from the riverbank, John could just make out a few wattle and daub houses, their thatched roofs pulled down like frowning eyebrows over the tiny open squares that were windows. A fire flickered somewhere and smoke curled up to join the mist weaving in and out of the bare rigging, hiding the top-castle from view.

Night was coming quickly but John could make out the heavy wooden spars and decking of a pier. He watched as the small boat and the Master between them manoeuvred the *Esperance* alongside. The mate called for fenders and two sailors brought loops of rope and hung them over the side. Others leapt on to the wharf and made fast to bollards standing like humped dwarves on the black planking. The crew winched a heavy stone anchor over the prow and the *Esperance* seemed to settle and sigh with relief at coming to rest in a safe harbour.

But was it so safe? John looked down at the man lying on the deck. He hadn't moved since he had fallen all those hours ago. Hairy Jack bent to feel his hand. It was stiff and cold and his eyes were still closed.

'He's gone,' muttered Jack. Another old sailor rolled the body on to its back and tried to lift the arms to cross them, but at an order from the mate they left the dead man and turned to their work. For a moment John stood, wanting to watch over the silent figure. It seemed wrong just to leave him there, but a warning look from Jack made him turn away.

He did his best to help while all round him the men set about getting the *Esperance* shipshape as best they could. On the falling tide, the hole in her side seemed huge and in places the rigging hung like the ribbons on a deserted maypole. Hairy Jack and Lou went aloft. John tried to climb with them but his foot was numb with cold. He slipped and Hairy Jack sent him down where he was less of a liability. Tired and dispirited, other sailors were not so patient with him and shoved him out of the way when he fumbled a rope or dropped a belaying pin.

At last the work was done. John watched as the Master spoke urgently to the mate. With an admonishing jab of his finger, he stepped over the side on to the wharf and vanished into the mist and darkness. The mate set a watch, men at bow and stern and another patrolling the deck. The others were free to sleep for a short time till it was their turn to watch, but instead they stood around restlessly, anxiously watching the shore for the Master's return.

Hungry and cold, John wondered if they would ever eat again, but after a while the sailor who sometimes cooked a kind of gruel and handed out dry tack began to forage in a crate behind the deck cargo. He pulled out some of the hard biscuits and shared them round. Like the others, John banged his biscuit on the gunwale to get rid of the weevils and ate hungrily. Then a crock of ale was passed around. Hairy Jack looked over at him.

'Best get some sleep, young Peg,' he said and nodded at the tarpaulin. John thought with regret of the long blue school gown he had left behind at the port. The Master had said it marked him out too much as a choir-school boy and had given him a short wool tunic to wear over his hose. Those he had taken off like the other sailors when they set sail, but at least they were safe in his tool bag. He ferreted around for them, pulled them on and burrowed in amongst the bales of fleece under the tarpaulin. Damp though they were, within seconds he was asleep and did not hear the Master's return, nor his angry words when he came on deck.

Chapter 3

There seemed to be a bustle going on somewhere. John pushed his head out from under the tarpaulin and felt his nose nipped by frost. It was very early, but the sun was shining and he suddenly felt that spring would surely be here soon. He struggled to his feet and looked about him, rubbing his eyes still misty with sleep. There was no one about but he followed the noise and hurried to the side of the ship. They were moored neatly against the wooden pier, close to some large sheds, their spanking new timber glowing in the morning light. Beyond, the little thatched houses he had seen from the *Esperance* the day before looked down on the busy scene, as if overseeing and approving the prosperity of the little harbour.

On the wharf, the men of the *Esperance* were busy with a long length of canvas. They were binding it tightly round something that lay on the planking. Hairy Jack looked up and called him over.

' 'Tis poor old Will,' he said, jerking a thumb down at the shape on the ground.

The sailors finished stitching Will's body into the canvas, sewing it neatly and strongly with a fine seam. They slung it from a pole then hoisted it clear of the ground between two bollards, where it swung very gently, as if the dead man were sleeping a last sleep in a hammock instead of on the bare deck under the stars.

'Buryin' will be later this forenoon,' said Jack. 'There's some already gone to tell the priest and dig Will's grave. They won't all go. Will was a Fairholm man. Only his mates from round 'ere will go, and any road, somebody got to stay and guard the ship.' He sniffed, cracked his knuckles and looked about him as if daring anyone to try and get on board.

'Will you go?' said John.

'Aye, I was 'is mate, and there's two or three more,' said Jack. 'There'll be some from Highwold, I daresay. There's none of them in the crew, mind, Fairholm and Highwold don't ship together, but they sort of call a truce together, like, when there's a death.' He crossed himself quickly, then nodded at the *Esperance*, snug against the wharf. 'But that won't stop some of the bastards from over this side tryin' their luck.'

'Stealing, you mean?'

'Pirates, the lot of 'em. And we're berthed amongst 'em. Not over there where we should be.'

John turned and followed Jack's pointing finger. Across the wide river were more wharves where ships were tied up.

'Why aren't we over there, then?'

'Just try lookin' again, young 'un.'

John gazed across, frowning. The river widened into a pool here, and the Fairholm bank was at least five ships' length away. After a moment he realized that the vessels in the quiet winter sunshine on the far side seemed deserted, no one moving about on board any of them. Many had their masts broken or gone, and none of them had rigging. And, when he really looked, he noticed that some seemed little more than wrecks, with great splintered holes in their sides and lying drunkenly in the water. Two had drifted loose and were keeled over in shallow water on long spits of sand further up the river where it narrowed a little. Like Will, they would never go to sea again.

'See them?' said Jack, nodding down the river.

'The sandbanks, you mean?' said John.

Jack nodded. 'Aye. All them sandbanks we passed on the way in is new. See, up till now, Fairholm was the port. The river-mouth led there direct from the sea. None of this nonsensical garbage of gettin' towed in to Highwold.'

'What happened?'

'There was a great storm. I did 'ear tell of it a while back, but I never knew it was this bad. But the sea has a mind of its own. And so does the good Lord.' He sighed. 'The sea took it into its mind to dredge up Fairholm river-mouth and move it up 'ere, to Highwold. So now . . .'

'Can it really do that?'

'If 'tis the Lord's will . . . if 'e do send a storm big enough.'

'But . . .'

'There's some 'ere in Highwold still sayin' it was Fairholm's wicked ways what done it. Lou heard 'em. They said Fairholm men do be proud, rich, arrogant swine. That they asked for God's punishment.' He crossed himself again and lowered his voice. 'Fairholm people do say it was the devil's work. That Highwold men are in league with the devil and they did make black . . .' his voice sank almost to a whisper, 'black magic to make a huge storm to take their livin' away. Jealous, see.'

John stayed silent. He looked across the river. The big sailor looked at the *Esperance* where the men were back on board keeping watch, though he could see neither the Master nor the mate.

Jack called to Lou. 'I'm goin' yonder,' he said, jerking his thumb towards the Fairholm side. 'See what's what. They'm still my folk, whatever . . .'

Lou nodded and turned to his work with the others, looking at the hole in the decking to see what needed to be done.

'Want to come, Peg?' Jack raised his eyebrows and John grinned. Jack led the way down a rope-ladder to a coracle moored by the wharf. The little craft wobbled alarmingly and he held out a hand to John to steady him. John crouched down quickly in the bottom, grabbing hold of the sides. The heights in the cathedral had never worried him like these boats did. They seemed to delight in rolling him about, ready to tip him out at a whim. At least the great church had kept still.

Jack pulled strongly to the far bank. They clambered out and between them pulled the coracle up past the water line, sticking the oars upright into the sand. Jack seemed to square his shoulders as he turned to look inland.

'Born and bred 'ere, I was,' he said. 'Everyone as I knew 'as long gone. I been all over . . . ain't been back in years, but some'ow you still belong. I 'ates to see it like this, I do.'

They climbed the sandbank and up on to what had once been a busy street. Deserted houses leant over the quay. A door banged gently to and fro in the breeze; seagulls perched brazenly on windowsills, gazing out to sea with brilliant, unblinking eyes. John peered in through a doorway. The room inside was bare. Nothing remained of the people who once had lived there. He was reminded of Aaron's house, looted and lonely after the Jews had been turned out of the city.

Hairy Jack swore. 'Them – them . . .' he said, unable to find a word bad enough, jerking his head towards Highwold across the rippling water, 'they'll 'ave stripped 'em all . . . taken all they can lay 'ands on.'

John frowned. 'Was everybody killed, then?'

Jack shrugged and moved on. 'Nay. Not killed. Well, some maybe, but most will 'ave moved on. Inland maybe, or to the top of the town.' He looked up towards a hill that sloped up beyond the straggling houses. 'But the port's done for. What'd they live on? No ships comin' nor goin'. No cargos, no work.'

'Couldn't they build everything again?'

'Nay, lad. Well, they could, 'course they could, but it's not worth the trouble. Not now God 'as seen fit to move the river-mouth. Not if everything 'as to pass through Highwold and pay for the privilege.'

He spat, noisily. 'Ships won't bother. They'll just put in to Highwold and unload there. Makes sense, dunnit? Not right, but it do make sense.'

They started up the hill, slipping and sliding on the loose sand that lay over everything in drifts. Far ahead, John could see the sails of the windmill and, beyond, the top of the church tower. That must be St John's, the church they had seen from the sea. Halfway up the hill, to one side of what had once been the road, was the beginning of a deep ditch. John peered over the edge.

'That was our defences when I was a lad,' said Jack with a rueful grin. 'Not much 'elp to 'em now.'

'Was that to keep the sea out?' said John, looking puzzled.

'Nay, to keep out them marauding devils from over yonder. And anyone else that cared to 'ave a go from the sea. And there's plenty of them, I'll tell you. Like them pirate bastards on the *Elephant* that was chasing us before.'

Pirates. So that explained the chase, thought John. Jack had a faraway look in his eye as they climbed on to the clifftop. The grass was longer here and green, and brittle dead leaves left from the autumn crunched under their heels. As they breasted the hill, the wind hit them and John staggered. Jack grabbed his arm and pulled him back from the sheer drop that seemed to open up at his feet. John steadied himself, shook his arm free, took a step forward and peered down, down, down to the pebbles below. A rich golden red and riddled with burrows, the cliffs were much higher than they had looked from out at sea.

'Rabbits?' said John, delicious thoughts of a rabbit stew making his mouth water. He had been hungry ever since they had left port.

'Plenty round about,' said Jack, 'but them burrows is most likely made by seabirds. That's where they nest.'

Just as John was conjuring up visions of fat yellow eggs sizzling on a griddle, Jack suddenly leaned further forward, straining to see below and away towards a huge heap of boulders and rubble leaning precariously against the cliffside.

'What . . . ?'

'What is it?'

'Look . . . look there. Look at all them people.'

Far below on the beach, John could see a small crowd of men, women and children. They were labouring with shovels, buckets and even with their bare hands. They had formed a chain from the edge of the sea back towards the narrow inland lake that led up towards the river-mouth and were digging up the sand and shale and piling it up on either side behind them.

'They're clearing the opening to the river. That great 'eap of rocks over beyond them must be where the cliff fell. This water close in 'ere, by the cliffs behind them sandbanks, that's the old river that led up the harbour, but it's got nowhere to go now . . . see?'

'But . . .'

'Aye,' Jack shook his head, 'but they'm whistlin' at

the wind I reckon.' He stood up. 'Still, at least they'm tryin' to do something, 'stead of sittin' about mopin'.' He brushed off his hands roughly. 'I'm goin' to give 'em a hand.'

'But what about the ship . . . our ship . . . ? And anyway, they can't really do it, can they? It's too big a job.'

'Worth a try, mebbe.' Jack stared over the cliff for a moment then glanced up at the sun. 'Come on, Peg, we best go. I'll come back on the morrow, when Will's safe at rest,' he said gruffly. He turned on his heel and strode away down the hill.

Jack's back grew smaller as he went down the hill with great leaps and bounds. John limped after him, stumbling and skidding on the dry sand that lay everywhere like dust. Suddenly, he caught his foot in a clump of grass and fell head first. For a moment he lay winded, then he rolled on to his back and looked up at the sky. A seagull wheeled over his head and hovered, screaming in the wind as if it were finding John's predicament the funniest joke. John glared up at it. He started to scramble to his feet, but as he pushed himself upright, he felt a hand on his arm. He gasped, lashed out and fell back on to the ground.

'Nay, brother, I'm sorry if I startled you. I was trying to help you to rise.'

John looked up. Above him stood a young monk, his arms tucked into the wide sleeves of his grey sackcloth habit as if putting them out of harm's way. His eyes were grey and the pale skin drawn tight over his cheekbones caved into gaunt grey hollows beneath them. His hood was down, showing the sparse hair round his tonsure already going grey at the temples.

He's from a church . . . The thought jumped into John's head unbidden and he drew back at the memory of other men of the church he had once known. But the monk simply looked down at him with a grave smile and John wondered if maybe some men of the church might not be so bad, after all.

'You are a stranger here.'

John gave a curt nod, licked his lips and got to his feet, flexing the ankle of his damaged foot.

'Are you hurt? In pain?' The monk knelt down quickly, holding out his hands.

'No,' said John, turning red and wishing the monk would get up. 'No, it's just my foot. It's always with me. I'm used to it. Please.'

'If you are certain . . . ?' said the monk. John nodded. 'If not, well, the Lord has taken away our dormitory, our kitchen and our – our church . . .' He lowered his eyes, his brow furrowed, then he looked up quickly. 'But our hospital is still there and we would do what we could for anyone who—'

'Taken away?'

'Perhaps God saw we had been given too much. The people of the town were – were very generous, but now . . .'

'But how was it taken away?'

'The storm. Our house, the house we built in the name of our blessed brother Saint Francis, stood close to the cliff edge.' He pointed far off across the cliffs. 'This part of the cliff close by did not fall. But where we were . . . are . . . was taken away in the storm.'

'You mean all those rocks and stones down there?'

The monk nodded, his chin lowered on to folded hands. Suddenly there was a roar from the bottom of the hill.

'I must go, someone's waiting for me,' said John, beginning to hurry away, then turning back still moving. 'I'm sorry about – about your house . . .'

The monk raised a hand, not a blessing so much as a farewell.

'I am Brother Edmund,' he called after John who was hobbling away at full speed down the hill. 'If you return, you will find us – the Greyfriars – at the hospital . . .' and his voice died away behind him.

John panted up to the coracle, which was already in the water, Jack paddling backwards to keep it close to the shore.

'Come on, come on, Peg-leg,' he said. 'Can't 'ang about all day.'

'Sorry, sorry, I was – there was a . . .' said John, breathless.

'Stow your garbage, lad, and get on board.'

Clogs and hose in his hand, John lifted his tunic and, swishing through the water, waded out to the coracle swinging in the current, straining to be away. Jack dragged him aboard, rowed swiftly to the *Esperance* and tied up beside her, muttering about nuisances all the way.

Up on the wharf the men and the mate were gathered ready for the funeral. Jack strode in among them and started to tell them about the people of

Fairholm and their battle with the sea. There were guffaws of disbelieving laughter that anyone should think they could dig a new river-mouth but one or two, Fairholm men themselves, promised to go with Jack after the funeral to do what they could to help.

'If God is with them, they will do it . . .'

'God took it away from them in their pride and arrogance,' said a Highwold man who had come for the funeral. 'Why should he give it back? They deserved what they got. For years they'd taken the plums of the trade round here, and now it's their turn to struggle and ours to prosper.' And he spat into the water.

The crew drew together, muttering and glaring at the man, but the tolling of a distant bell took their attention. Lou and another man lifted Will, still swinging gently on his pole. They hoisted him on to their shoulders, and the small procession slowly started away from the river in the direction of the sound. John could see no one left on the *Esperance*. He remembered his tools under the tarpaulin. What if . . . ? He pulled at Jack's sleeve.

'Now what . . . ?' Jack shook him off impatiently.

'Will my tools be safe?'

'No one'll touch 'em with a funeral on,' he said. 'They wouldn't dare. And the mate'll stay on board I daresay.' Then suddenly he paused, struck by a thought. 'Nay, Peg, bring 'em along. You bring 'em. Go on.'

John clambered quickly over the gunwale, groped under the tarpaulin and drew out the bag. He slung it over his shoulder and hurried, dot-and-carry, to catch up the straggling group of men. Someone started up a dirge on the penny-whistle and, sadly and slowly, the procession wound its way towards some distant trees.

They drew closer, and John saw that the trees were enormous; giant beech trees. A few dead leaves still clung on to branches swaying in the wind high above, spreading moving patterns over bare earth flecked with moss. On every tree, the tip of each twig held a tiny, tight bud that glistened in the rays of the winter sun. As they walked, John became aware that they were no longer passing through a straggling wood, but that the trees had gradually parted to make a long, imposing avenue in front of them. On either side was forest, full of shadows, but ahead, in a clearing at the top of the long avenue, lay a small chapel nestling amongst smaller trees, its thatched roof making it seem as if it, too, was growing, part of the wood in which it stood.

The ceremony was short. John watched, head bowed, as Will was placed in the earth and his grave covered with a few branches picked up on the walk through the wood. He tried hard not to think of another funeral, of a bier holding Hugh, his friend, a small figure bound with white cloth from which yellow curls had escaped and bobbed about full of life, it had seemed, as the funeral procession left the cathedral. John blinked hard, swallowed and pulled his mind back to the present. The men were singing a farewell hymn that only the sailors knew. He couldn't join in, but at least it was unfamiliar and held no memories.

'Who will carve the tree?' called a voice.

A Fairholm man volunteered but Jack put up a hand.

'Nay, let the young 'un do it. Peg's a proper carver. Do a good job, won't you, lad?' he said to John.

'Carve? What tree?' he said. 'What do you mean?'

'Didn't you see 'em?' said one of the crew. 'Come and take a look.' The men crowded round the nearest tree and pointed upwards. There, carved into the bark above his head, John saw a little ship looking like a miniature *Esperance*. Its bow was tilting up towards the sky as if breasting an invisible wave. The initials BH were carved beside it. As they moved from tree to tree, there were more and more tiny vessels, some with initials, some without, floating across an ocean of beech trees, headed out towards the sea.

'All sailors is buried 'ere,' said Jack, 'specially if they did die at sea and their bodies is saved. And every one 'as 'is ship nearby.' He nodded at the little fleet of carved boats. ''Tis tradition.'

John stood entranced.

'Well?' said Jack. 'You goin' to stand there all day? Your turn, Peg. Ye ain't much of a sailor but you'll carve our Will a ship fit for an admiral, eh?'

John nodded, still looking up at the little carvings. The men chose a tree that was bare of ships and, with a grin, John dumped his bag on the ground and took out his mallet and chisel.

'How long'll it take?' said Hairy Jack.

'Till evening,' said John.

'I'll be back for ye.'

John was already sizing up the tree and drawing a pattern ship on the bare earth to work by. Jack chuckled.

'You'll do better 'ere than on the ship, I reckon. Land legs you've got,' he said, 'but a good pair of 'ands, I'll grant ye,' and he turned to join the procession already beginning to dance and caper on the way back to the wharf. John smiled to himself, sweeping the bark of the great tree clear of lichen. No weeping and wailing, he thought, more a celebration, but who would want weeping and wailing with a ship carved on a tree to remember you by?

As the procession disappeared up the avenue into the wood, the wind sighed and the branches creaked, but John, immersed in his work, was oblivious to everything. He didn't see the shadow moving between the trees. He didn't hear a horse's hooves stamping quietly on the soft moss under them. He didn't see the dark, inquisitive eyes watching him intently as the little vessel took shape under his hands. He didn't hear the rustle of the leaves as the eyes narrowed and the owner darted away like a wraith through the wood, nor the soft drumming of the hooves gathering speed into the distance.

Chapter 4

The men returned for him just as John was putting the finishing touches to the W for Will. They were raucous and merry from Will's farewell revel. Red noses glowed and the knotted beech tree roots came in for many a curse and a kick when the men stumbled and fell as they staggered through the wood. But at the sight of John's beautiful little ship carved into the trunk of the huge old tree, they sobered up in astonishment. He might not know a shroud from a ratline, but he could surely make boats in his own way.

No one seemed to know if Will had another name, so the W was left on its own below the delicate carving. John's ship, looking very like the *Esperance*, seemed to dance along on the bark waves. Overhead, the branches of the great trees were intertwined as if to shield the tiny vessel from the wind and rain in a way that had never happened for any ship that Will had sailed in when he was alive.

The men thought John's carving wonderful. He had even put a tiny figurehead on the prow of the little vessel, no bigger than his little fingernail.

'You've given 'er a wee angel,' said Hairy Jack,

smiling and rubbing his hands. 'That's good, lad, that's very good. Saint Nicholas would like that. That'll take proper care of poor old Will.'

He jerked his head back towards the graveyard and the others nodded, crossing themselves hastily in a blurred, rather sketchy kind of way. Lou slapped John on the back and he looked pink and pleased, polishing his tools and putting them away carefully.

'Best get on back then,' said Jack. ' 'Tis gettin' dark and there's only the mate left on board. Once it's dark, funeral or no, that lot'll be on board afore ye can spit.' He jerked his head again, this time down towards Highwold and its citizens.

They moved together down the avenue of trees, still stumbling a little but this time because the shadows were lengthening and the gnarled roots truly difficult to see. The brief jollity of Will's farewell gave way to sombre faces and an anxiety to return to the *Esperance* before more damage could be done to her, or their few belongings stolen.

As they climbed on board, John saw that the Master was there. He looked thunderous and the mate had his whip handy. The men hurried to their watch or to find a sheltered place to sleep. But the tarpaulin was tightly battened down now, with no room to burrow in amongst the bales. The Master and the mate had been busy while they were all in the woods and the party was definitely over. John sat huddled together with Lou and Jack for a while as the stars came out and the frost returned.

Presently Jack began to snore where he lay slumped against the mast and, at a barked word from the mate, Lou lumbered to his feet. He stretched and scratched himself and started to patrol the deck, his eyes alert now and fixed on the shore. Another sailor took the river side of the ship, keeping a watch for intruders that might come quietly up the side from a boat with muffled oars. John sat leaning uncomfortably against a crate, his tool bag wedged under his knees, his eyes beginning to droop.

Suddenly he became aware of a shadow looming over him. His hand went to his tool bag and he pulled himself upright. His mouth opened, ready to yell.

'Hush!' A hand went over his mouth. 'Over here.'

John calmed down as he recognized the Master's voice. He was pushed towards the stern-castle and up the ladder. The Master squatted on a small keg and pulled John down beside him. He put his face close to John's and spoke in a whisper.

'There is trouble.'

John looked round quickly but the *Esperance* lay quiet on the river, the black water beginning to glint with silver from the rays of the rising moon. A seabird cackled briefly and was silent. Nothing moved except the two men on watch, slowly pacing the length of the ship.

'Nay, the trouble is not on board,' said the Master, 'not yet. But we need repairs and we will be in trouble if they are not done. I want them done in Fairholm.' He nodded towards the far bank. 'There are still men over there who will do the job for a fair rate and who need the work, God help them. Not everything was lost, they could still do what needs to be done . . . not build a ship perhaps, not now, but repairs . . . But these thieving devils this side want a king's ransom just to let us go and tow us across.'

'Couldn't someone just – just row across and get help? Hairy Jack and me – we . . . we went over this morning.' John hesitated, unsure of whether they had been wrong to go.

'Poor innocent,' said the Master. 'It is easy enough for one or two of the crew to go on a jaunt, but the Highwold men know who is who on board the *Esperance* by now. If I go, they will follow me and then the ship will be lost. I've managed to stave them off for a while, but only a while. Thieves that they are, I need money to pay them for the tow, and then more for the repairs in Fairholm. I must have money, the good God help me, and soon, or the cargo will be worthless.' He looked away into the distance, then glanced down at John, lowered his head and rested his chin on his hands, his elbows on his knees.

'You're a sensible lad.'

'Sir.'

'So it will be you I send.'

'Send me, sir? Send me where?'

'To find Sir Richard Elleston. He is my friend. We started life together in the same household but we have gone – well, we have gone our separate ways. He has prospered and I . . .' The Master dropped his head.

'You're the Master of a great ship, sir.'

'And I am tossed on the waves as she is,' said the Master with a brief smile. 'Always at the mercy of the next rich man to hire me and always at the mercy of God and the sea.' He sighed. 'But we are all at the mercy of God, and Sir Richard will have his troubles now with the harbour gone. But all his eggs are not by any means stored in one basket and I have found out that he is not far away. No one would tell me where, but I believe his house may still stand over yonder, though it may not be habitable. No one would say. Perhaps they don't know and anyway, I would not trust them whatever they said. But Fairholm men will tell you where he is.'

He looked at John again and put a hand on his shoulder.

'You must go now, John.'

'Now, sir? But it's the middle of the night . . . How will I find him in the dark? There will be no one about.'

'I know. There is an early curfew over there, I believe, to keep what little is left in safety. I will take you across now while no one over here suspects what we are trying to do. I have a coracle ready. Hide up somewhere till morning and then set about finding Sir Richard. Sir Richard Elleston, remember. I know he will help.'

'How much must I ask him for?'

'Nay, lad, you must not ask him for money. Not directly. You must tell him I am here and need to see him urgently. He will understand what that means, I'll be bound. Ask him to come as close as he can to the ship without being seen. Then you will come to the riverbank in broad view and signal to the watch to fetch you. In the meantime, I shall put it about that you have run away. That the sea was too much for you . . . some such tale. When you appear, you have changed your mind about leaving, could get no work, something like that, you understand? Then I will send the coracle over for you. You must not be seen with Sir Richard. I will find some way of meeting with him once he is found and close by.'

'And, sir, what name will I give him? To say who you are?'

'Tell him Godfr— nay, simply tell him, the Master of the *Esperance*. He will know. Now. Are you ready?'

John nodded. The Master hesitated.

'John, I am sending you for two reasons.' He smiled apologetically. 'One is that you are of little use on the ship. The others are rough men but they know their trade. They can at least do a little by way of repairs while we are waiting – some of the rigging maybe. And it is possible that Sir Richard would not agree to see a seaman he didn't know. Even on board a ship, Saint Nicholas would not take you for a seaman and neither will Sir Richard.'

John gave a wry little smile back at him.

'But the other reason is that I trust you. I think you are an honest boy and will not betray me. But I must ask you. You will not run away? Find a new life on shore? You will not forget about Sir Richard and what we need?'

'Nay, sir, I promise. And you forget why I'm here. My friend . . . my friend Aaron may be somewhere in Flanders – where, I don't know. But I want to find him and you said you would take me there. You will take me, won't you?'

The Master nodded gravely. 'God willing. But, John, whatever you may think, it will be tempting once you get on shore to . . . to . . . John, I am going to ask you something you will not like.'

John looked up at him with a puzzled frown.

'I want you – I want you to leave your tools with me. To make sure you do come back.'

'No!' John took a step back, turning red with anger and dismay. 'I thought you trusted me. I gave you my word. Isn't that enough?'

The Master looked into John's furious eyes. He sighed.

'I could make you leave them,' he said, 'but I will not. Better a willing messenger than one with a grudge. Come. Fetch your tools. The coracle is just below and the river is rising.'

John crept back to the mast where he had left his tool bag. He took off his clogs and hose and stuffed them in it. The bag rattled just a little as he lifted it and Hairy Jack stirred.

'You all right then, young Peg?' he muttered. John grunted and the big sailor went back to sleep, still heavy with ale from the funeral revels, his black curls under their bonnet cradled in the crook of his huge arm, the fingers with their nails like horn curled up like claws.

The Master waited till Lou was leaning over the gunwales to peer out among the shadows on shore. The other look-out was in the prow, his eyes raking the sandbanks to watch for moving craft. The Master slipped quickly down the ladder, held out a hand first for the bag and then for John, and pushed the coracle silently away from the side. John watched the moon riding along beside them, lighting a long

44

pathway up the river. It seemed impossible they would not be seen, but the Master rowed swiftly and noiselessly with oars muffled with rags, so that they seemed little more than a phantom slipping through the water. At the other side, John scrambled out and splashed ashore. He squatted down and felt about in his bag.

'Sir!' he called in a breathy whisper.

The Master paddled backwards, holding the coracle in place against the running tide. 'Hurry, what is it you want?'

'Here!' Holding out his hand, John paddled through the water up to his ankles.

'What is it?' The Master sounded impatient.

'It is my pledge that I will come back,' said John. Into the Master's hand he placed his little stone angel, half finished but still unmistakably an angel and something he would never, could never leave behind.

The Master nodded. 'I understand,' he said. 'Thank you, John. I will take the greatest care of it.' He nodded again and placed the little stone figure gently in his lap. 'God be with you. Go now.' He turned the coracle and was away across the river like a leaf on the tide.

John dried off his feet as best he could with a cloth from the tool bag he kept for polishing tools and put on his hose and clogs. Struggling up the hill through the sand would not be easy in the dark, even with the moonlight, but he didn't relish the thought of the damp, dreary, deserted houses down by the river.

He set off up the hill, his bag over his shoulder, stopping every now and again to get his bearings. At the top, he expected the wind to burst on him as it had that morning with Jack, but the air was still. He turned to the left.

'Larboard . . .' he said to himself with a smile and then added, '. . . I think.'

Suddenly he stopped. What if he happened on the cliff edge? In this light, he might easily miss it and go over before he knew it, plummeting down the steep sandy precipice, bouncing from ledge to ledge in a shower of red dust to certain death below. He shivered and carried on, his foot paining him now and dragging him back.

He came to the place where he had met Brother Edmund. Here, the path forked, one way carrying on along the clifftop, the way the young monk had gone. The other tipped down over the hill into the darkness. If what was left of the monastery was straight ahead, perhaps that's where other houses still remained, Sir Richard's among them. He thought the derelict windmill must be up that way somewhere.

He edged forward, then stopped. A cloud swallowed the moon and the world went black. He waited for a moment, straining his eyes to see ahead, but the moon refused to come out again. Somewhere to the left was the cliff edge. He thought it still to his left. But what if the line of cliffs wasn't straight, but curved round and was ahead of him now?

Throwing down his bag, he felt around him for a dip in the ground. His fingers met coarse grass. The saw edges would cut deep if you slid your fingers along them, like tiny wicked daggers in the sandy soil. But a little to one side, the ground became kinder. The grass was softer, brown and brittle but yielding, and a couple of tough-leaved bushes gave a little shelter. He took out the old cloth, wrapped it round his shoulders, laid his head on his tool bag and tried to sleep.

Chapter 5

John was awoken by a hand on his shoulder. He sat bolt upright, ready for trouble. The thin, grey face of Brother Edmund was looking down at him.

'Twice now I have frightened you. I am sorry. I happened upon you while I was walking. I did not like the thought of you sleeping out here in the cold, alone.'

'I'm ... I'm ... all right,' said John, but his teeth were chattering. He knelt up and stuffed the polishing cloth into his tool bag.

'Here,' said Brother Edmund, 'take this.' He held out a crust of bread and a small piece of cheese, more rind than anything. John took the food gratefully and gobbled it down.

'Will you walk with me?' said the monk.

'Where are you going?'

'Back for the Morrow Mass. Dawn is breaking, it will start soon.'

'Is your church – well, your hospital – is it near the part of the town that wasn't swept away?'

'On the very edge. Not far away there are still some houses left, thanks be to God.'

'Then I will come with you. I am looking for . . . for . . .'

'Looking for someone? We know the people of the town. Many are gone, but some have chosen to stay. May I ask – whom do you seek?'

'Sir Richard Elleston.'

The monk looked away for a moment and John could not see his face.

'I see. No, he is no longer in the town. His house was lost, though much of his land remains. They say he is still close at hand, though I have no knowledge of his new dwelling. But there are people in the town who can tell you, maybe. Come. I must return to prayer.'

They set out along the clifftop, the stars fading as dawn broke grey and misty over the glimpses of windswept water John could see through the slender, damp-blackened trees. Constant driving wind had bowed the trunks till they leaned in away from the sea, their fragile branches reaching out as if seeking someone, something, to make the wind stop and let them stand upright. The monk was tall with a long stride, but he glanced down at John's foot and slowed a little.

'I can keep up,' said John, his jaw jutting. 'You don't have to slow down for me.' Brother Edmund nodded, smiled a little and quickened his step.

After a while, ahead of them, John saw the trees give way to open grass where a low stone building stood, solid and somehow comforting in the faint glow from the rising sun. But then he noticed how close to the edge of the cliff it stood and that one end of the building was little more than rubble and the debris from loose mortar, strewn about on the grass. Further away, a high stone arch lofted against the lightening sky. On one side was a wall. On the other was space where the wall had tumbled over the cliff.

Brother Edmund noticed John's intake of breath. 'Aye,' he said, 'it is precarious indeed. Perhaps we shall not have even the hospital for much longer. Another storm, even a small one, and that will be the end. But it is as God wills.'

'Is that your hospital?' John nodded towards the low building.

'It is. The rest has gone. Will you come and pray with us, my brother?'

John hesitated. There was no time for prayer; he must find Sir Richard Elleston as soon as he could. But Brother Edmund seemed to read his thoughts.

'It is still very early. Many of the people will not even be astir yet. You may not be welcome at this hour. Welcome in this town is not – not what it used to be . . . though – though I'm sure they do their best, poor souls.'

They walked a little closer. Outside the building a small group of monks gathered in their grey habits – Greyfriars, the brothers of Saint Francis. Brother Edmund led the way towards them, and as they turned to face him, John felt suddenly shy. Their gaze was so direct, so open. Brother Edmund greeted them and put out an arm to welcome John in.

'A traveller,' he said.

'You are welcome,' the murmur ran amongst the brothers, but they wasted little time on ceremony and started the ritual of the Morrow Mass where they were, standing in the open air. Almost without thinking, John joined in the Latin he remembered from hearing the men choristers and the canons at their devotions. Brother Edmund looked up and smiled, but when the service was over he asked no questions. John was ready to answer how he came to know the Latin so well, but it appeared that the Greyfriars felt no need to ask questions except those needed for the healing of the sick. Their concern, he thought, was not the affairs of other people, only the affairs of God.

After the Mass, several of the brothers went to the ruined end of the building and started to roll and heave some of the stones lying about, sorting them into sizes, putting them on to already formed heaps that stood well away from the cliff edge. The monks were gaunt and thin, and it looked as if it was as much as they could do to haul them across the grass, let alone lift the heavier ones. John resisted an urge to go and help them. He must find Sir Richard Elleston, tempting though it was to stay and feel the joy of working with stones again.

The door of the hospital opened and a single monk came out. John saw him pause and wash his hands in a bowl of water on the ground outside the door. Behind him, a man closed the door gently, but not before John had seen his face. It was inflamed and misshapen, flaking with loose skin and blisters. His reddened scalp showed through tufts of hair that stood upright as if stiffened with grease. He stared briefly at John through swollen eyes, then pushed the heavy door shut. A leper. John shivered. He knew about lepers. There had been a leper hospital outside the city he had left, but those he had seen had not looked as – as sick as this man. Brother Edmund looked at him intently, his head a little on one side.

'Aye, those are the people we care for,' he said. 'Before the storm, there were many in the town who gave us alms, money and food, to help our work. Now, they cannot afford to do so, so we beg where we can. We hope to give them spiritual sustenance in return. We are the only ones here to tend their souls now that the priests from the church have gone.' He raised his eyes in the direction of the church tower in the distance.

'The bread you gave me . . .' said John, uncertainly.

'That was given in answer to my prayer,' said the monk.

John reddened. 'But you needed that . . .'

'And so did you. Think no more of it. But when you can, remember and do likewise.'

'I couldn't do what you do,' said John, glancing at the hospital door. The monk smiled and shook his head, as though to say that was not to be expected.

'But I can come back and help you with the building once I have found – found the person I am looking for.'

'The Lord would welcome extra hands for his work.'

'I know about stones and cutting them. I have my tools,' and he gave his tool bag a gentle rattle. Brother Edmund looked surprised but still asked no questions.

'I will come back,' said John, 'when I've . . . done what I have to do. There will be time while the ship is repaired.' He stopped quickly, aware he might already have said too much. 'My name is John,' he said, changing the subject. He hesitated. 'But they call me Peg,' he said, looking up with a half-smile. Brother Edmund looked puzzled, followed John's eyes down to his foot, put an arm round his shoulders and gave him a brief hug.

'John is a fine name,' he said. 'He was Our Lord's beloved friend.'

The other brothers had dispersed, some to the hospital itself, some to continue prayer in the shelter of the hospital wall. John saw that a little way off through the arch there were houses, larger than those down by the river. Some of them had smoke coming from the chimney hole in the roof. That meant people were up and about. He must go.

'God's blessing be with you, John,' said the monk, seeing John was really on his way this time.

'And with you. And thank you.'

John hurried away through the archway with his dot-and-carry gait, carrying the feel of Brother Edmund's arm round his shoulder with him. Somehow it gave him strength and quietness, the kind of feeling he hadn't known since Aaron and his father had disappeared, and before that, his own father . . . But he turned his thoughts away from that dark place and concentrated on keeping his footing through the knotted grass and then the rutted cart track in the middle of the lane.

At the first house, he got short shrift. An old

woman with a broom swept him away with a gruff 'No beggars here'. Did he look like a beggar? He didn't think so, but he tugged up his hose, straightened his tunic and ran a sleeve over his face just the same. A small crowd of people carrying wooden buckets, shovels and picks came towards him up the path. They wore rough working clothes and one or two had jerkins made of skins. Some shoved past him roughly without a glance but others stared at him and hurried on, hugging their tools against them as if afraid he might try to take them. He turned and watched them as they followed the path through a field towards the cliff edge where it dipped down towards the beach. Tagging along at the back of the group was a boy of about his own age. The boy stopped, glanced after the others, then came back to John.

'Who are you? What you want? We got no food nor nothing.'

'I know,' said John. 'I wasn't going to ask.'

'Well then?'

'I'm looking for someone . . . Sir Richard Elleston. I'm told he lives here – or did.'

'What you want 'im for?'

For a moment John was stuck for an answer. He certainly would not tell him the story, but nor did he want to anger the boy by telling him to mind his business.

'I – I've been sent to find him,' he said finally, 'that's – that's all I know.'

'Don't believe you. You must know what ye want 'im for.'

John paused for a moment and decided against giving battle. Instead, he tried a hesitant kind of grin.

'I'll wager you know everyone in the town, don't you? I'll wager you know where I'll find him? Go on. Tell us. I'll get larruped else.'

The boy eyed him suspiciously then suddenly grinned back.

'Over there, look. That 'eap of rubble. That was 'is house. Was. It ain't on the cliff edge so it never went over, but it fell down in the storm. Sir Richard's gone over to Eastwych to stay with 'is cousin.'

'Eastwych . . . is it far?'

'Half a day's walk mebbe. Set off now, you'll get there by dinner. If there is any dinner. Better than staying 'ere, any road, we've none 'ere.'

John nodded. 'Which way?'

The boy pointed out a lane between the houses that petered out into a narrow path and disappeared over a low rise. On its way, it seemed to turn and lead back towards the river.

'That's the Eastwych path. You got to cross the river but the ford's beyond Highwold, so you shouldn't meet too many of *them*,' and the boy spat copiously on to the ground.

One of the people disappearing down the path to the edge of the cliff let out an angry yell. The boy gave John another quick grin and ran after them. John watched them for a moment, wondering if Hairy Jack would really go and help them in their endless task of digging a new river-mouth through the sand, and if they would succeed. He turned on his heel and set off down the lane.

He was hungry now, but on he went. The houses were mostly empty, all the people gone to the beach. It would waste time to try to beg for food. Once in the fields, he passed an orchard with a few rotting apples lying on the grass left from the harvest. He picked them up gratefully and ate what he could of them. After what seemed a long time, he saw the river ahead of him, and away beyond it, in the distance, what he thought must be the beech wood where his little ship sailed on the great tree. He wished he had his angel with him. His foot ached, so he sat for a while on a stone in the wintry sun, rubbing it, preparing himself to ford the river. The sea was cold, but the river would be icy with water down from distant hills.

'What have you done to your foot, boy?'

John wheeled round. Standing behind him, not five feet away, was a girl. At least, he thought it was a girl. She wore a gown but it was shapeless, just caught loosely at the waist with a belt and ending almost at her knees, the way no girl he had ever seen would wear such a garment. Over it, her sleeveless skin jerkin made her even more shapeless. Her hair was hidden by a man's hood and she wore clogs like his own over thin leather slippers. But her face was small and fine and her eyes were dark and brilliant.

'Well?' she said, imperiously. 'Are you going to answer or are you dumb?'

'You startled me.'

She laughed. 'That's not an answer, boy.'

In spite of being so taken aback, John laughed too. 'My foot is . . . well, it's always like this.'

'Were you born like – like that?'

'A twister? A dot-and-carry? A peg-leg?'

The girl dropped her eyes for a moment as if offended at the words. Or perhaps, John thought, at the possibility of being in the company of such a person. Then she looked back as if daring him to read her thoughts. He gave a little smile and went on.

'No, it was an accident. It happened a while ago and far away from here. Sometimes it hurts more than others. I've walked a long way.'

'I know.'

'What do you mean, you know?'

'You came from the beech woods.'

'Nay, that was yesterday – but how . . . ?'

'I watched you carve the little ship.'

'How did you . . . ? I didn't see you there. Were you at the funeral?'

She shook her head and the hood slipped a little, showing thick dark plaits wound tightly round her head.

'Nay. Sailors' funerals are no place for a *girl*.' She spoke with a bitter little twist to her words, but then she sighed. 'I watched from a distance . . . as usual. I seem to watch everything from a distance.' She gave her head a little shake as if shaking the thought away. 'I went back this morning to see the little boat on the tree, but you had gone.'

'I went to Morrow Mass with the Greyfriars,' he said. 'Then I walked here.'

'The Greyfriars!' Her face lit up. 'That's over at Fairholm. You were there?'

'My Master comes from there,' said John. 'He has sent me to – he has sent me on his business.'

'But you live at Fairholm?'

John shook his head. He was not about to tell this girl, whoever she was in her strange peasant clothes with her far from peasant voice, any more of his story. Well, not now at any rate. He looked at her.

'I must be away,' he said, 'or my Master will be angry.'

'But who is your Master? And where—?'

'Nay, that's enough,' said John. 'I have to get to Eastwych before dark.'

'That's easy,' she said, 'you can come with me.'

John sighed. 'I haven't time—'

'Come with me, I said,' she cut in briskly. Behind her, a little way off under some trees and cropping the scant grass lazily was a chestnut pony. 'I live at Eastwych. It is only a mile or so beyond the ford. Come.'

John looked round but there was no one else about. She was out alone. He could hardly believe it. There must be other riders, servants, someone near to look after her. She ran to the pony and took its reins. John, limping along behind her, attempted to help her into the saddle but she shook him off impatiently, stuck a foot into the stirrup and sprang up. To his horror, she flung a leg over the saddle and sat astride.

'What's the matter, boy?' she said.

John couldn't find an answer.

'Well, if there's nothing the matter, get up behind,' she said. 'I can take you to Eastwych.'

Ride behind her? Ride behind a young girl like

this on her own? If they were seen he would be in terrible trouble.

'Well, would you rather walk?' she said, tossing her head.

'It's not – it's not – seemly,' he said.

'Not seemly! There is a great deal that I'm told *is* seemly that is also very stupid,' she said. 'I am tired of it. Get up behind me.' She sighed. 'I will put you down long before you are seen, if that's what is troubling you.'

She stared down at him and a smile twitched at the corners of her mouth. 'Not afraid, are you?' she said. John shook his head. 'Well then . . .' and she shook the reins gently. Swallowing hard, he put his foot in the stirrup and swung himself up behind her.

'You'd better hold on,' she said. Blushing scarlet, he shoved his tool bag between them, held her round the waist as lightly as he could without falling, and with a click and a 'hey up' they were away. They splashed through the ford, the hem of her gown getting well and truly soaked, but she took no notice and they galloped on towards the distant tower of the church at Eastwych.

The path swung round to the left round the bottom of a low rise. At the top was a gaunt wooden structure, its crossbeam reaching out like a blackened arm. It creaked mournfully as they passed it, giving it a wide berth, and the little horse shied away with a whinny.

'That's the town gibbet,' the girl flung over her shoulder. 'They hang people there. It marks the bounds between Eastwych and Highwold.' John looked up, shivered, and turned his head away.

Well outside the town gate at Eastwych was another horse with a groom, idling away his time beside it, whittling on a stick. At the sight of them, he ran forward and pulled John roughly from the pony.

'Mistress Christina, what are you thinking of? Who is this?' The groom whipped out a knife and held it to John's throat.

'Nay, you oaf, leave him. He is a – a guest . . . a traveller, anyway. Leave him alone, he is harmless.'

'That's the last time I lets ye go on your own, Mistress Christina. Master will be—'

'The Master will not know, will he? Will he, Finn?' The groom looked sulky and sheathed the knife. 'This – this boy is looking for . . .' She looked down at John, still gripped by one of the groom's sturdy arms. 'You did not say for whom you were looking,' she said, her face haughty but her eyes laughing at him. She would find out his business now and she had known it all along. John pulled himself free.

'Sir Richard Elleston,' he said, angrily. 'I am looking for Sir Richard Elleston who is said to live in Eastwych.'

'So I believe,' she said. 'You had better come with us.'

John tried to wrench his arm free but the groom held on tightly and the girl said nothing to make him let go. She took the reins of the second horse and led the way towards the town. Furious, John stumbled along after the groom through the town gate and into a wide square of fine new buildings, mostly wattle and daub but one or two of wood with black oak beams. At the far end, behind another high wall, stood a large stone house with tall, narrow glass windows. The gates stood open and through them John saw a steep outside stair leading up to a heavy wooden door studded with massive nails. Smoke came out of two separate chimney holes in the roof and at one side of the building was a wide path that led behind it to some outhouses sheltered by pine trees. The girl slid from her horse and walked the two animals into a stable.

'Stay there,' she called over her shoulder. 'Wait. Finn, let him go, you dolt. He won't run away. And anyway, fool, I told you, he's a guest.'

The groom, apparently taking no umbrage at the way she had spoken to him, still looked suspiciously at John. He let him go with a surreptitious shove and brushed off his hands down his sides. John glowered at him and stood shouldering his tool bag, changing it back to the other shoulder, fidgeting in irritation. The groom said nothing but stood calmly as if used to waiting, picking at his teeth with a bit of twig.

After what seemed a long time, the stable door creaked open and the girl came out and stood in the entrance. John stared. It was as if the sun had suddenly come out and dazzled him. Gone were the rough clothes, the hood and the jerkin. In their place was a brilliant yellow gown trimmed with white fur. Over her thick plaited hair was a translucent gold veil that hung to her shoulders. She laughed.

'Close your mouth, boy,' she said. 'It is rude to stare, so I am told. *Unseemly.*'

John closed his mouth and swallowed. Without a glance, she strode past him. Then she turned. 'Finn! The horses!' With a reluctant glare towards John, the groom went into the stable and shut the door.

'Well, are you coming?'

'I have to find Sir Richard . . .'

'You have already told me that. Do you think I am an idiot?'

'Clearly not,' said John, his temper rising again. Why did she think she had the right to insult him like her servants? He clamped his jaw tight, determined to resist the sparkle in her eyes.

'Well, then,' she said and swept towards the house and up the stair, lifting her skirt a fraction. At the top, she turned, her eyes still full of laughter.

'Oh, come now. Just where do you think you are more likely to find the whereabouts of this Sir Richard? In here – or out there?'

The door opened and suddenly the laughter left her. She turned and stalked in, leaving the door ajar behind her. With a furious kick at the ground that stubbed the toe of his good foot, John stumped up the stair and followed her inside.

Chapter 6

In spite of the windows, the great hall was dark after the bright winter sun outside. Huge blackened beams crisscrossed the ceiling high overhead and clean rushes covered the floor. A fire burnt in the fireplace at the centre of the room, flickering shadows into corners. John looked round for the girl but she had disappeared. He stood uncertainly for a moment. A serving man closed the outer door softly, then passed behind him and left by another door at the far end of the long room.

John hesitated, then moved as if mesmerized towards the fire. Such warmth! He couldn't remember sitting by a fire since a time that now seemed long, long ago ... He dropped his tool bag on the floor and squatted down, holding out his hands towards the flames.

'Cold, are you?'

John looked up. These people did not waste words, he thought. Above him, at the top of a short, steep, narrow stair, a big, burly man stood with his hands on the rail, his heavy legs apart. John stood up, hoisting his tool bag over his shoulder. The man descended slowly and deliberately, taking his time to come down to John's level. They looked at each other across the space, then the man strolled over to him.

'Sir Richard Elleston.' It was a statement, not a question.

'Yes, sir.'

'Why do you seek him?' So the girl must have gone up those stairs and told this man about him.

'I seek him for – for my Master.'

'And who is your Master?'

John knew there was no point in prevaricating with a man in whose house he had no place and who could keep him here a prisoner if he felt so inclined. The servant who had just left would be one among many.

'He is the Master of the *Esperance*, sir.'

'A ship's master. I see.' The man walked to the fire and held out a casual hand. Unused to the heat, John's head began to swim a little and he longed to sit down. The man chewed his lip then seemed to make a decision.

'Sir Richard is my cousin . . .'

'Oh!' John heaved a sigh of relief. 'Is he here then, sir?' he said, eagerly.

'Nay, he is from home. He was here. He came to us after the storm but he has . . . affairs to attend to – elsewhere. He has been gone some time and we expect him daily.' He gave John a level look. 'Your Master's errand is urgent, I take it, yet he sends a lad. Why did he not come himself?'

What side in the quarrel between Fairholm and Highwold did Eastwych people take? Or perhaps none? The Master had not prepared him for this.

'He . . . he . . .'

'Well?'

'The *Esperance* is damaged . . . quite badly. He didn't want to leave her.'

'She is at Highwold.' Again, not a question. John nodded and the man smiled a little to himself and turned away. 'No, he would not want to leave her there.'

John still couldn't tell what the man was thinking.

'Well, you will have to wait here. Go to the kitchen. They'll feed you and you can sleep with the servants if my cousin does not return today.'

'Thank you, sir.' John turned towards the door to follow the servant but the man's voice stopped him.

'What is in the bag?'

Automatically, John clasped it tighter.

'My tools, sir.'

'Tools, eh? Ship's carpenter, are you?' said the man, with an ironic twist to his voice.

'Nay, sir, apprentice stonemason.'

'Apprentice stonemason?' The man sounded astonished. 'What is a stonemason doing on a ship?'

'The Master was giving me passage to Flanders. I was looking for . . . for a friend who went there, I think . . .'

'You seem to spend your days looking for people.'

John sighed and dropped his head. 'So it seems, sir.'

'Hmm . . .' The man was about to speak when there was a bustle at the top of the stairs. A young boy came bounding down, followed by a woman in a blue gown, carrying a large bundle. The boy wore a short sword at his waist and a fur travelling coat slung over one shoulder. At the bottom of the stair he flung the coat on to a wide stone window seat and strode towards the man by the fire.

'Father!'

'You are ready, my son?'

'Sir.'

John stared at him, astounded. Was this a boy . . . or was it the girl who had brought him here? The same bright eyes, the same fine bones, the same heavy dark hair but shorter, curling in to his neck . . . the same way of moving, quick, assured, imperious. The man clapped a hand on to the boy's shoulder and they went together towards the outside door. The woman followed. She paused to pick up the coat from the window seat and laid it carefully on top of the bundle.

'Finn will go with you. Is that company enough? I cannot spare . . .'

The boy nodded.

There was a sudden patter of feet and a rush of yellow down the stair. Her skirt lifted almost to her knees, the girl who had brought him here hurled herself down the stairs and across the room towards the boy and his father.

'Nay, Finn is my servant. Why must he go? Father, you promised.' The girl's voice was high with anger.

'Christina, be quiet. Be still. Think what you are doing, girl. Have a care of your garment.'

She stopped, breathing heavily. She flung the stuff of her skirt away from her, shoulders tense, eyes blazing, drawing herself up straight and lifting her chin.

'Your brother has need of Finn. I wish Finn to go with him. He will return in a few days. Someone else can have equal care of your horses.' Her father cocked an eye at her. 'You know my feelings, Christina. It is time you stopped riding about the countryside with just a servant. I have allowed you far too much freedom. It is unheard of in other houses and it will stop in this one. You are turning into nothing better than a – a trollop.'

Furiously she opened her mouth to join battle, but her father broke in.

'Enough, Christina. I warn you.' He flexed his shoulders and took a deep breath but his gaze was inflexible. 'Now. Christopher is leaving us till the summer. It will be many months before we see him again. Let him leave in peace, girl.'

He turned away from her impatiently. The woman looked at the girl and gave an almost invisible shake of her head. Christina subsided but still looked mutinous. She swept back her skirt and marched over to the woman.

'Mother, let me take those for you,' she said and took the bundle, dropping the coat on the floor.

'Have a care what you are doing, Christina,' said her father, angrily. 'I believe you are becoming not just a trollop but careless in your household duties and a scold to boot.'

Again the girl's head went up and her mouth opened to speak. This time her mother laid a gentle hand on her arm. 'Peace, child,' she said quietly. She touched her cheek and the girl dropped her head, taking the woman's hand and holding it for a moment. The woman released herself gently, bent to retrieve the coat and put it round the boy's shoulders.

'Here, my son. You will need it on the journey. It is still very cold in the mornings.'

John suddenly realized he should not be witnessing this private family scene – but if he moved now it would remind the man he was still there. He stayed very still in the shadows as the boy kissed his mother on the cheek, then turned to Christina.

'Twin, be easy. Better not to . . .' He glanced at his father and back at her.

Suddenly, she threw her arms around him and John saw tears glistening in her eyes. 'Christopher, oh Kit, I shall . . .'

'Hush. Christina, I will miss you too.'

'Why are you going so soon? Usually you stay much longer.'

'Our father has willed it, Christina. Hush now. Truly, I will be back before you know it.'

He held her away from him at arm's length, pressing his fingers into her shoulders and shaking her gently. 'In the meantime . . .' He shook his head, looking at her anxiously. She nodded, shrugged and turned away towards her mother, biting her lips.

'Come,' said their father. He put an arm across the boy's shoulders and went with him to the door. Christina went to follow but once more she felt her mother's restraining hand and stayed where she was, brushing an angry arm across her face to stem the tears.

At the door, Christopher turned, gave a brief wave and clattered down the stairs with his father. From outside came the sound of horses, shouts and laughter and finally the clatter of hooves across the square, growing more and more distant.

Christina gave a great shuddering sob. Her mother placed her arm around her shoulders to lead her back upstairs.

'Come, child, up to the solar. Only my women are in our chamber and I will send them away. You can recover yourself there.'

As she turned, Christina caught sight of John, still waiting by the door to the servants' quarters.

'You!' she said. 'You saw me . . .'

Furious again now, all tears vanished, she hurried up the stairs and crashed shut the door at the top behind her. Her mother gave John a puzzled look, then followed Christina on silent slippered feet. With a last glance at him through the crack, quietly she closed the door again.

John slipped away. On the other side of the servants' door at the far end of the hall were more stairs leading down to a yard. There he found another stone building a little way away from the main house and set at right angles to it. Nervously clutching his tool bag, he put his head round the door. No one seemed to notice him so he stepped inside and waited, looking round.

Thankful that Finn was not there, he approached a man winding a carcass of beef on a spit over an open fire. The smell in the kitchen was heady and the heat tremendous. John felt giddy, and when he put up a hand to brush away a bunch of prickly herbs dangling from a beam to dry, he felt himself reel and stumble. He half-fell against the man at the fire who glanced up with a curse and shoved him away. Dropping his tool bag, he steadied himself on the stone of the fireplace. An old woman pounding leaves at a table dropped her pestle and came shuffling over to him.

'Nay, lad, tha'art sick.'

John shook his head and allowed himself to be settled on the floor by the fire, leaning against his tool bag. She touched his cheek and the back of his hand.

'Shrammed, then.'

John looked up enquiringly, but the old woman simply took a bowl and a wooden spoon, ladled some broth from an iron pot hanging over the fire and gave it to him with a lump of black bread that she took from a crock on a windowsill. John ate hungrily. Whatever 'shrammed' was, this was an excellent cure. The broth was thick and oily, with carrots and bits of meat floating in it. John sopped it up with the bread, tipped the bowl to swallow the last drop and licked his fingers.

'Better, lad?'

'Thank you. Much better.'

The old woman's smile was more gum than yellow tooth, but John smiled back. The man at the fire muttered to himself and shot him a baleful glance.

'What's up with you, William,' she said, 'ye get fed well enough.' The man spat into the fire.

'I've to stay here till Sir Richard Elleston returns,' said John. 'I hope that will be . . .'

'Whatever the master do say,' she said with a shrug of her rheumaticky old shoulders, and went back to her pounding. 'You can bed down in the outhouse along of us.'

'If ye're to stay, ye'll earn your keep,' said William. ' 'Ere. Take a turn at this.' He let go of the iron handle and jerked a thumb at the carcass of beef. John scrambled to his feet, tired still but feeling some energy beginning to stir. He took the handle and started to turn it, finding the spit heavy and stiff. The man laughed, spat again, this time at John's feet, and slouched out.

The old woman shook her head. 'Lazy vermin,' she said with a sniff. ' 'E'll get out of work if 'e can and swear the devil's a Christian.'

'I don't mind,' said John. 'Best to have something to do.' He went on grinding the handle round and round. 'I've worked on a ship. That's hard too,' he said, remembering his arms aching from heaving on sail and anchor and then the sick feeling in his stomach. At least the floor kept still here.

'Oh aye,' said the old woman. She glanced at the door. 'You – you'd best keep an eye out for that William,' she said. 'Nasty tempered lout, 'e is. And whatever ye've got in that bag, take care of it.'

John looked at her with an enquiring tilt of his head, but the old woman was paying attention to him no longer and was standing with one ear thrust forward to hear something going on outside. William hurried back into the room, full of malicious glee.

'Young master's gone,' he said. 'Finn went with 'im. Master went to see 'em on the way but now 'e's back, there's the devil of a scuttle between 'im and young mistress. Mistress is wailin' and wringin' 'er 'ands. Master swears 'e'll beat the young 'un till she'm chastened.' He laughed and blew his nose into the fire. 'That'll learn 'er, proud she-cat as she is.'

'Shut yer vile mouth, William, ye – ye . . .' The old woman gave a small cry of disgust and jabbed the wooden pestle in the air towards him. 'Wish someone would beat *you* . . . I'd do it meself with pleasure if I still 'ad my strength.'

'Aye, but ye ain't, old woman,' said the servant and stuck two fingers up in her face. John felt his own fingers tighten round the spit handle, but the old woman muttered and turned away with an angry shake of her head. William hawked and spat, and scratching himself energetically, lifted the tail of his tunic towards the fire and stood warming himself. He looked at John with a self-satisfied sneer.

The kitchen became full of bustle and noise as the dinner was prepared. More servants appeared and great dishes and platters were carried from the kitchen, across the yard and up the stair to the great hall. John helped, taking bowls of food that would not spill when he limped. He waited at the top of the stair for a steward to direct the serving men to take them from him to the table.

When John peeped into the hall from the stair, he saw the top table standing on a dais, already laid with knives and trenchers. In the centre, in front of the high-backed chair of the master of the house, stood the salt, its stand of precious metal glinting in the candlelight. Smoke wreathed from the hearth among the high beams overhead. People were already seated and the food was passed among them.

'For Sir Basil,' came an order to one servant and 'for Lady Elizabeth' came another as the best of the food was offered first to the master and mistress of the house, then along the top table to the younger children, their chaplain, their steward marshal and Lady Elizabeth's waiting women. Down the descending tables below the salt, lesser folk in the household were given meaner fare.

John went a little further into the room at the steward's direction. He stood holding a bowl of codling apples that smelt of autumn sunshine. As he gave them a secret sniff or two, he noticed that there were two empty chairs at the top table. The first, on Sir Basil's right hand, John thought must be Christopher's chair, kept for him till his return. Further along, on the left of Lady Elizabeth, was another space. The girl, Christina, was missing too. With a shock, he realized he was disappointed not to see her, even if those eyes had been laughing at him, standing there holding a bowl of apples just like any other servant. He took another sniff of the apples. What did it matter if she wasn't there? He looked back at the table. Perhaps Sir Richard had returned by now. He thought not, though to be sure he didn't know what he looked like. Passing over the empty chair, he turned his attention to the rest of the company.

But after a moment, he sensed rather than saw a movement at the top of the stair behind Sir Basil. He looked up. Staring at him through the half-open doorway from the solar was the girl. She stood very still and there was no question that her gaze was on him. It was almost as if she were trying to say something to him, but what? And why should she?

Without thinking, John took a step forward. A servant cannoned into him and in saving himself trod heavily on John's injured foot. The pain was excruciating. John gasped and let go of the bowl. The servant managed to save it, though one or two apples dropped and rolled across the floor among the rushes. The steward hurried over and grabbed the bowl.

'Get you gone,' he said, harshly. 'Go back to the kitchen and stay there.'

John hobbled to the top of the stair to the yard, trying to restrain hot tears of pain and humiliation. He glanced back. The eating went on undisturbed, the altercation apparently unnoticed, and up above, the door to the solar was closed and Christina gone. Had she seen his clumsiness? He felt he couldn't bear it if she had.

'Useless gimp, you are,' jeered William, when John returned to the kitchen. 'I knowed that, soon as I seen you. Pain in the arse, that's you. Cripple. Shouldn't get no dinner, I reckon. Good for nowt.' But at a glance from the old woman, sitting on a stool by the fire, the other servants left him alone and he was allowed to share their food without much more than a 'hey up, Peg-leg ... put yer foot in it well an' truly, then'.

Later, he was offered a share of one of the wide straw-filled mattresses in the servants' quarters where they all slept together, but preferred to curl up on his own on the kitchen floor. His foot hurt and what with fleas and snoring, he would be restless and perhaps keep the others awake. Nor did he relish the thought of perhaps having to sleep next to William.

Some time after midnight, he stirred and rolled over. Something was wrong. There was a faint swish. Something, someone was creeping about in the rushes. Whoever it was stopped and waited. John kept very still and steadied his breathing, deep and even, so his visitor would think him asleep. After a while, the shuffling started again and through shuttered eyelids he saw a silhouette crouched down, coming towards him. He tensed himself, waiting. When the figure was close, a hand reached towards the tool bag at John's head. John lashed out an arm, caught the figure by the wrist and yanked it hard. The man fell back over John's legs and he kicked him away. The light from the fire caught the face ... William. He had thought it might be.

The servant struggled up, swung round and lunged for John's throat, but John put up his arms and shoved him off. William stumbled and fell into the embers of the fire. He yelled, and by the time John had realized what was happening, scrambled to his feet and pulled him away, William's tunic was scorched and smouldering. John reached up to the beams overhead and grabbed a cloth hanging up to dry. He started to beat at William's clothes while the servant lay screaming and swearing.

'Be quiet,' said John, 'for Jesu's sake, shut your

mouth. The whole house will be raised. You're not hurt. The fire is out. It's just your clothes scorched a bit, that's all.'

He pulled William to his feet and turned him round to make sure his tunic wasn't still alight. A great brown scorch mark covered the back and as John brushed it, it started to crumble. John grinned to himself as the man's flabby backside was exposed.

'I hope you've got more clothes,' he said, trying not to laugh.

William snarled and jerked himself away.

'I'll get even with ye,' he said, 'don't you fret. I'll get yer.'

'Get me?' said John. 'What for? You were trying to steal my tool bag ... or look in it, anyway. And I stopped you from burning.'

'Aye? Is that 'ow it was? I don't think so. I come in for a warm, to get by the fire an' ye went for me ... rolled me into the hearth an' tried 'oldin' me down in the flames. That's 'ow it happened.'

'Who's going to believe that?' said John. 'Why should I try to burn you?'

'Oh they'll believe me, all right,' said the servant with a sly grin, 'an' even if they doesn't, I'll get ye somehow, just wait.' He spat on the floor towards John and stumbled out of the door into the night.

Chapter 7

Sleep wouldn't return. The ash from the fire, disturbed by the scuffle, tickled his nose and he sneezed, four, five, six times. He rubbed his nose to stop the itch and felt the sweat running down his face. He needed some air, some clean, cool, sweet air.

Sound carried at night. If he tried to leave by the heavy kitchen door, he might be heard from the outhouse where the servants slept. But in the kitchen there were no glass windows and the shutters by the bread crock hadn't been properly closed. He climbed quietly on to the sill and, hefting his tool bag behind him, slid down on to the ground only a few feet below.

Outside, the moon was up and shining clear and cold across the yard. The frosty air nipped his nose and he took a deep breath, feeling life go tingling through him. He stretched and wriggled his shoulders and his toes. All this heat must not be good, he thought, makes you soft, makes you idle. William's arms were strong enough but there was still something soft about him.

Animals in the outhouses stirred and coughed. Somewhere in the distance a fox barked and he heard rats scuttling among the bones and garbage in the midden. 'Stow your garbage, lads,' he thought with a sudden pang. There was nothing soft about Jack or any of them on board the *Esperance*.

He walked silently across the yard, behind the main house to the far end where high up, dark, shuttered windows gazed across the top of the outer wall to a scattering of houses gathered under its protection. The tower of a brand new church glistened in the moonlight, an ugly gargoyle gaping its open mouth to the stars. John smiled. How he would love to have carved that monstrous little creature. His smile faded as he remembered the stone angel. He hoped the Master would keep that safe at any rate. He sighed. He trusted the Master, but things happen . . . he wished he hadn't left it. He wished he had it here. But he knew that if it were here, William would try to steal it, damage it, do it some harm, just to get his own back.

'Boy!'

John started, catching his breath. He whipped round, peering among the shadows, left, right, back again . . . but everything was still except for a horse stamping in its stall away at the back of the kitchen. He could see no one, yet someone had whispered something, he was sure. He listened. Silence. He was about to turn and go back to climb in through the kitchen window, when a low giggle came from above. He looked up.

Christina sat leaning on a windowsill with her hands in front of her mouth to stifle her laughter, her fingers laced, pressed against her lips. Her hair fell forward, hanging in long waves down to her waist. Her white night shift, gathered up to her neck, seemed almost dazzling in the moonlight. Her eyes sparkled. She raised a finger and mimed 'ssh', then opened her hand, palm towards him, to say 'wait', and disappeared. When she returned, her hair was pulled back with a cord and her night shift covered with a skin jerkin. She hoisted herself on to the window ledge, and stood up.

John watched her, dismayed. She couldn't be going to jump?

He blushed suddenly at the sight of the night shift caught up round her waist under the jerkin. Her legs showed almost up to the knees, as they had when she was riding, but now there were no hose even, just bare flesh. She threw down her clogs on to the earth at his feet with a faint thud, waited to make sure no one had heard, then sat, legs dangling over the edge, gripping it with her fingers.

'No!' John let out a whispered cry. She let go and flapped her hands frantically at him, shaking her head, teeth bared, face furious. John held up his own hands and closed his eyes. He would say no more. She glanced over her shoulder, rolled on to her stomach and reached below her with one slippered foot. The foot found a stone protruding from the wall and she put her weight on it, then stretched sideways to another stone further along. John held his breath as she let go, pushed her weight across and grabbed the next windowsill, neatly changing feet on the stone as she did so. John calmed down a little. She must have done this before. He watched fascinated as she edged along the side of the house, dropping lower and lower through a series of random stones set sideways into the wall till she was within jumping distance of the ground. She landed at his feet with a superior smile and a toss of her head.

'That was . . . that was . . .' He wanted to say 'stupid' and 'wonderful' at the same time but she broke in quickly.

'Easy,' she said, her voice low, though her expression spoke volumes. 'It was easy. Now, I'll tell you what I want.'

'What do you mean, what you want? I haven't got anything to give you,' said John. 'Anyway, how did you know I would be here?'

'I don't want *things*,' she said, scornfully, 'I have enough of those. And I didn't know you would be here. Of course I didn't. I would have found a way to speak to you somehow, but when I happened to wake up, I thought it would be a good moment. I wished very hard for you to come and you did.'

She spoke in such a matter-of-fact way, as if people always came just when she wished, that John blinked and waited. She pushed her feet into her clogs, walked across to the stone mounting steps by the wall and sat halfway up them, her back very erect, arranging the skirts of her night shift over her knees with great propriety.

'You can sit here,' she said, less of an invitation than a command. John squatted on the bottom step, since she had taken care that there was no room beside her. There was a moment's strained silence, then:

'I want you to be my groom,' she said. 'Finn has gone with my brother and I must have someone I can – I can . . .'

There was a pause.

'Trust?' said John, looking up at her. When he met her eyes, suddenly she looked anxious, vulnerable. 'What makes you think you can trust me?'

'I – I don't know,' she said, leaning down a little towards him, 'but . . . but I can, can't I?'

She held his gaze, blinking a little, her shoulders stiff, her fingers twisting so tightly that the knuckles shone white. Almost at once, before he could speak, she straightened up again. But it was enough. She was not the iron-hard little tyrant she appeared. Something was hurting her. She was pleading for help without being able to ask. She caught his eye again and he knew that he would refuse her nothing. He only hoped she would ask nothing he should not, ought not agree to.

He said as lightly as he could, 'You want to go riding on your own still, is that it? Like when I was with you yesterday.' He tried a smile. 'What makes you think I won't tell your mother . . . or your father . . . ?'

'You would have told them by now if you were going to,' she said. Suddenly, she whipped round and stared at him, round-eyed.

'You won't,' she whispered, 'you won't tell him, will you?'

'No, I won't,' said John, resisting the temptation to reach up and touch her arm to reassure her. 'But how did you know I wouldn't?'

'I heard you talking to my father. You didn't want to tell him about the message to Sir Richard and you didn't. You didn't blabber . . . you didn't let anything out by accident . . .'

'He didn't try very hard to make me.'

'No . . . If he wanted to, I think he could make you.' John dropped his head. 'Yes, he probably could.'

'But he doesn't know about me and . . . and the riding on my own. He thinks Finn stays with me. So he won't ask you that, will he? He trusts Finn completely and Finn's wife was my wet nurse so he is almost family . . . not quite, of course, they do not come to dinner with us, but . . .'

John nodded. 'So that's why your father lets you go with him.'

'I tell you, he doesn't know I'm left alone. Nor about my clothes. He thinks I ride side-saddle like a proper lady should . . .'

'He hasn't seen you come back?'

'Oh yes, many times. But I usually change saddles like I change my clothes, away from the house. There is a hut in the woods, but sometimes it is locked and I – we have to take a chance and come back to the stables as we did yesterday.'

'And Finn allows you to do this?'

'Allows? He's a serf. He doesn't *allow* me anything . . .' she said looking at John in amazement, the imperious young mistress returning. Then she dropped her eyes. 'He – he doesn't like it but I . . . persuaded him,' and she gave John a smile that would have persuaded the Archangel Gabriel. 'Anyway, I know that he goes poaching from time to time, so persuading him was not – that – difficult,' she said with a giggle. John smiled.

'And how will you – persuade – your father that I am to be trusted as Finn is to be trusted?'

Her face clouded over. 'I don't know yet,' she said, 'but all I know is that either I will have to go riding side-saddle with my mother's waiting women or else it will be someone repulsive like – like William. And I can't . . . won't face that.' She sat forward, her elbows on her knees, her chin on her hands. 'I can put my father off the William idea. I shall say he ogles me and is obscene – which he is sometimes . . . not directly but it is in his eyes, I can tell. But the waiting women are another matter. Puddings!' she exclaimed in disgust.

John laughed, then glanced up at the windows, suddenly serious. 'I'm sure your father will say no,' he said, shaking his head. 'I can't imagine how you will persuade him. But . . .'

'But if I can?'

'I am not the rider that Finn is and I have never had the care of horses . . .'

'Oh pooh, there are grooms in plenty in the stables to take care of them,' she said airily, 'but I think my father likes you . . .'

'But . . . ' John looked at her. That was the sort of thing she might say just to make him do what she wanted. 'I was only with him for five minutes,' he said doubtfully.

'After he had spoken to you, when he came up to the solar, he said you were a "stout young fellow" . . . that's praise from him.'

'Hmm. I don't think that means he would let me take you riding on my own,' he said. 'He won't allow it, Christi—' He stopped himself, quickly. She hadn't told him her name herself, so perhaps he ought not to use it. 'He won't allow it, I'm certain.'

She sighed angrily and scratched with her fingers at the moss between the stones on the steps, crumbling it and letting it drop.

'It isn't fair. My brother can do anything . . . anything he likes. My father adores him . . . lets him have what he wants, go where he wants, do what he wants . . . but I am his twin . . . his *twin* . . .'

She was almost shouting and John put out a hand to quieten her, drawing it back quickly before he touched her arm. She covered her face, then sat back, looking into the distance, pouting.

'I should have been a boy,' she said. 'I'm his twin but not *quite* . . . not *enough* . . . I should have been a boy too. It isn't fair . . .' and she started picking savagely at the moss again, her head buried in her chest, muttering almost to herself.

'Christopher can go and be educated at a great household while I have to stay at home . . . He can ride astride while I have to jog along side-saddle like a ninny . . . He can have Finn with him whenever he wants while I have to make do with – with . . . He can learn to handle a crossbow and a sword while I sit with a needle and thread . . . He can have clothes you can move in while I have to wear cumbersome skirts and cover my hair . . . it isn't fair . . .'

All this had been in her head a long, long time,

thought John. He bit his lip. 'Is there nothing you are allowed to do that he isn't?'

She shook her head. 'I'm even beaten more often than he is.'

'Beaten?'

'My father says I need chastening, that I am brash and rude and full of phlegm and that it must be beaten out of me before I am unmarriageable. Well . . . beating me won't make any difference because – because unmarriageable is exactly what I want to be.'

John laughed.

'It's true,' she said, 'it's not a joke.'

'I didn't think it was,' he said, 'it's just the way it sounded.' Then he said, serious again, 'But, beaten . . . You are beaten?'

'Girls are beaten too, just like anybody else. Well, girls like me . . . some stay at home as they should.' She put her head on one side and spoke in a sing-song voice. 'They learn to keep the linen and make the medicines. They learn to command the servants and obey their husbands. They learn to be good wives. Good wives!' she said, almost spitting, her face screwing up, disgusted. 'And I must marry who he says . . . someone I don't know perhaps . . . anyone he chooses . . .'

John looked troubled. She looked at him and shook her head. 'My father is not a bad man, he is a good father. I suppose some would say it is me that is bad . . .'

'No,' said John, shaking his head emphatically, 'not bad, but just . . . well – different . . .' and he smiled.

She shrugged and then managed an uncertain little smile back. He looked up at the darkened windows of the house. Nothing stirred, but at any moment someone might miss her and come looking, and the open window was very obvious.

'Listen . . . I'll do what you ask,' he said. 'If you can persuade your father to let me ride with you, of course I'll do it, but I can't think that it'll happen.'

She stood up, towering over him as he sat on the steps. She looked away and smiled. 'That's settled, then,' she said and her smile broadened and turned into a pleased little hug together of her shoulders. She started down the steps and John scrambled out of the way. At the bottom, she turned and looked at him.

'What is your name?'

'John,' he said, surprised that she didn't know it already. He thought for a moment and then said, almost shyly, 'They – they call me Peg . . .'

'They?'

'Oh . . . people I – I used to know. I – I'm on my way to find one of them but . . .'

'Why Peg?'

He said nothing but looked down at his foot with a short laugh, his mouth turned down at the corners. She dropped her eyes for a moment and he thought he heard her say, 'Oh, I see.' After a moment she said, 'Who are you looking for?'

'A friend. He was badly treated too, but different. He had to go away or they might have killed him. He was – he is a great friend. I miss him. It's important to find him.'

'More important than—?' She broke off suddenly. She swept across the yard to the wall, hoisted her skirts and started to climb.

Halfway up, she lost a clog. It slithered and clattered down the wall and he held his breath. She paused for a moment, looking up at the window, but no one came and she continued on, nimbly stretching out, taking her weight, changing her foothold. She reached the window and eased herself backwards to sit on the sill. Then she drew in her legs, stood inside the room, leaned out and threw down the other clog.

'Goodnight, Peg. Be *my* friend,' she whispered, rapping her chest with a finger. She withdrew swiftly into the darkness and quietly closed the shutter.

John looked down at her clogs lying at his feet. At least she hadn't expected him to climb up after her to give them back, but they couldn't stay here. She must have known he would pick them up. She would have so many other pairs that servants, even her mother, would never miss them, but finding them outside . . .

John picked up the clogs and stuffed them in his tool bag. He would find a way to give them back to her later. He had no doubt she would find a way for there to be a 'later'. He went back to the kitchen and climbed through the window seconds before the old woman shuffled in to make up the fire.

Chapter 8

John grew restless. Still Sir Richard did not come. He saw nothing of Christina and he doubted that he would. He filled in the time helping the old woman in the kitchen.

'Old Nance, they do call me,' she said, popping a titbit made from a strange concoction of herbs into John's mouth, her bones seeming to clatter together inside her with laughter at the face he made.

'So long since I been called Old Nance, can't call to mind what me real name might be.'

John looked at her wrinkles and her whiskery chin and wondered what she might have looked like before she was Old Nance, when she had a name of her own. What had he looked like before he limped and people had called him Peg? Already it was difficult to remember . . . the limp was so much a part of him now, and the sudden pain that came and went.

'Some call me Peg,' he said.

'Oh aye,' she said, pounding away at some small brown berries that gave off a brackish smell, 'but not all . . . ?'

John shook his head, firmly. She nodded, a dewdrop from her nose joining the shiny heap of berries. 'Just twixt us two, then,' she said and she smiled her gummy smile.

For several days, John found excuses to work in the stable with the horses too, so he would feel more at ease with them if the time ever did come for him to ride out with Christina. He watched out for William who was often there, whistling through his teeth as he rubbed down the horses. He must be better with horses than with people, John thought. All the while, William kept a sly eye on John and John took care they were never alone together. He wasn't afraid of him, but he didn't want any trouble that might mean Sir Basil would send him away before he could meet Sir Richard.

When he still did not come, John began to wonder if he should not go back to the *Esperance*. But if Sir Richard came while he was gone, what then? Had the Master realized he might have to wait and wait like this? He fretted and grew more anxious as the hours passed.

No summons came from Sir Basil or Christina for him to go riding with her, as he had been sure it would not. Nor had he found a way of returning her clogs to her and they stayed in his tool bag. He only caught sight of her once, dressed in a heavy riding gown, her hair covered with a fur-lined hood, sitting side-saddle between two of her mother's women, her face a picture of sullen defiance. She spotted him at once. Her eyes narrowed almost to slits as if daring him to laugh at her, so he gave an almost imperceptible shake of his head and quickly looked away.

And then, without warning, there came the sound of jingling harness across the market square, then hooves on the cobbles through the entrance gate and excited voices hallooing. John was in the kitchen and heard the commotion in the distance. He looked up at Old Nance.

' 'Tis 'imself back again,' she said, delight dancing about in her faded eyes.

'Himself?'

'Sir Richard Elleston, my lord's cousin.'

John breathed a sigh of relief then immediately started to feel anxious in a different way.

'What is he like? Is he – is he a good man? Will he . . .'

'Sir Richard? He'm as good as gold, my duck, but it ain't just that. It's the news 'e brings with 'im – that's what'll be good . . .' and she rasped her stiff hands together happily.

'What news is that?' said John. It couldn't be anything to do with the *Esperance*, surely.

' 'Tis not for all ears, mind, Peg. She don't know 'erself yet, but Sir Richard's been gone to settle a 'usband for the young mistress.'

'For Christina?'

'Mistress Christina,' she said sharply, 'aye, for the young mistress.'

'Mistress Christina,' he said hastily. 'But – but she'll hate being marr—'

' 'Ow would ye know?' William's voice, oozing curiosity, came from the open door. John whipped round, feeling himself go red.

' 'Ow would ye know if she'd 'ate bein' wed?' said

William again, quietly this time and coming into the room, close to the fire, his shadow looming large and crooked on the rough stones of the wall.

'I don't,' said John, hastily. 'I mean . . . well, I just thought she's – she's young yet, isn't she?'

'Plenty old enough to be betrothed,' said Old Nance, nodding wisely. 'Daughters of nobles like Sir Basil, they can be betrothed at seven or eight years old if their fathers do wish it. 'Tis often done.'

'Taken a fancy to 'er yerself, 'ave yer?' said William, scratching his belly through the gaps between the fastenings where they didn't quite meet.

'No,' said John, 'no, I have not,' and he flushed with sudden anger.

'What you gettin' red in the face fer, then, gimp?' said William, suddenly pushing his own face close to John's so John could feel the spittle on his own skin. John returned the glare, wiped a hand hard down his cheek and turned away with a 'tchhh' of disdain. William turned to Old Nance, his eyes full of malicious glee.

' 'Ear this then,' he said, 'Finn just told me that she'm cuttin' up good and proper . . .'

'Mind yer mouth, William,' said Old Nance. 'If ye means the young mistress, then say so.'

William laughed. 'Yeeeer,' he said, tipping his nose with the back of his hand. 'Young mistress she may be, but she'm rantin' and yellin' and pullin' 'er 'air something terrible, Finn do say.'

John kept his face turned away so they should not see the distress in his eyes. This was just what she

91

had dreaded, and it had happened so quickly after she had told him.

'Reckon she'm for it,' said William, eyes still on John. 'That little rump'll be good an' sore this time . . .' and he licked his lips salaciously. John caught hold of the spit handle, his knuckles white, but William's eyes were on him. He saw the look on John's face and smirked. 'Told you . . . fancy 'er yourself, don't ye . . . don't ye?'

But Old Nance caught him sharply across the back of the legs with a broom handle.

'I'll not 'ave that talk 'ere,' she said. 'Ought to be ashamed. That's the young mistress you're talkin' of . . . you'll 'ave some respect while I'm 'ere.'

William shrugged and turned away. 'Thought that'd get 'im,' he muttered, then raised his voice over his shoulder to John. 'Don't you worry, I'll get ye again an' I'll be ready for ye, peg-leg an' all, gimp . . .' and he shambled off out to the yard, with a quick rub of the back of his legs as he went.

John let out a sigh and pressed his knuckles together. Old Nance glared after William.

'No respect,' she said, 'no respect for anyone. Take no notice of 'im, Peg. I don't know why 'e do 'ate you so, but 'e do. Just you keep away. Keep a distance.'

John nodded. So Old Nance didn't know of the fight by the fireside then. She turned to the pot over the fire, lifted out the ladle, blew hard and supped up a noisy taste of the broth. With a satisfied little nod, she returned the ladle to the pot, running her tongue over her lips and chewing at them with satisfaction.

'I daresay we'll be losin' ye soon, then, my duck, now Sir Richard's come back,' she said.

'Will they send for me?' John said, anxiety returning. 'How will I know when to go and see him? Will Sir Basil remember with all – all that going on?'

Old Nance thought for a moment. 'Mebbe not,' she said. 'Just to make sure, best go an' see Sir Richard for yourself at dinner.'

'Oh but . . .' John glanced at her, biting his lip. 'Last time I spilt the apples and . . .'

'You don't need to serve at table,' she said with a little cackle, 'best not, I daresay. But ye can go to the great 'all come dinner time and they'll see ye and remember. Go on. They can't bite you, ye ninny.'

So John went up the stair to the great hall, threading his way among the sharp elbows of the servants. Sounds of great merriment wafted out to him on tides of delicious smells. Tankards clashed together, voices bellowed rude songs or belched deeply, hands beat on the table or clapped shoulders. John stood awkwardly at one end of the hall. At the other, at the top table, sat Sir Basil. None of the women were there. Next to him in Lady Elizabeth's place sat a slender, fair-skinned man, blue-eyed, his hair as flaxen and straight as Sir Basil's was dark and wavy. Was this Sir Richard or was it the man on the other side of Sir Basil in Christopher's place?

As John studied the second man, his heart sank. Either this was the man he had to have dealings with or else, worse, far worse, he was to be betrothed to Christina. Either way, surely, lay disaster.

The man was pinch-faced, with small black eyes set close together beneath eyebrows that met in the middle. His thin hair straggled to his shoulders. He drummed his fingers on the table impatiently, as if he was waiting for something to happen. He did his best to respond to the celebrations around him, but John thought it was a struggle. He had a sinking feeling that the man's face wasn't used to smiling.

Suddenly Sir Basil spotted John.

'Boy!' John hurried up to him. 'Not now, boy – we are celebrating my daughter's betrothal to Lord Lovat.' He nodded towards the fair handsome man beside him then waved a hand towards the other. 'You will speak to Sir Richard tomorrow.'

The pinch-faced man looked at Sir Basil then back to John, an enquiry in his eyes, but Sir Basil continued without explanation.

'We hunt as soon as it is light. Sir Richard will see you on our return. You will not be forgotten.'

'Yes, sir. Thank you.'

Still looking faintly puzzled, Sir Richard nodded, giving John no more than a glance. Disappointed, John stumped down the stair. Now that Sir Richard had come he was impatient to give him the message from the Master and to be away. He was not looking forward to the meeting. Sir Richard looked as if he might be difficult to deal with. Still, all he had to do was deliver the message and be gone. At least it meant that the man Christina was to marry was, well . . . not so bad, at least to look at.

The hot kitchen was more than he could bear. He turned along the back of the house to get some air before trying to sleep. He thought longingly of the calm of the hospital and the Greyfriars, probably kneeling for the last service of the day under the first star. Even the lurch and lunge of the *Esperance* and the cold night air at sea seemed better than the steam and stale smells of the kitchen. He slumped down at the bottom of the mounting steps.

'Peg! Peg!'

He jumped up. Christina was at the window. Even in the fast-fading light he could see her face was blotched and swollen from crying. Her call to him was half whisper, half sob.

'Did you see him? Did you see that – that – creature they would marry me to?'

'Yes, I saw him. Christina, he – he looked . . .'

'Never mind what he looked. You don't know what he did.' She took a deep breath, trembling at the memory. 'Before dinner, in front of everyone . . . *everyone.*'

She looked down at John, her eyes full of fury, her fists clenched, beating on the sill. He shook his head and held up his hands, trying to calm her, quieten her.

'In front of everyone, when we had only just that moment been presented – he kissed me. Not my hand, not my cheek even, but on my mouth as if I was his already. His chattel . . . his – his . . . He is disgusting . . . disgusting . . . pigswill . . .'

Again she banged her fists down hard on the stone sill, sobbing in fury. John stood feeling helpless. Only once had he felt such a tide of emotion within himself, when the crowd had attacked Aaron's house. They had led Aaron's father away tied by the neck like an animal and pelted him with stones.

John could do nothing then and he could do nothing now. He wanted to put a hand on a shoulder to comfort her, but perhaps it was as well she was up at the window out of reach. She would only have pushed him away. After a while, she steadied herself and looked down at him, her eyes huge with pain and anger.

'I am to marry him next month – next month – sweet Jesu, what am I to do? I couldn't bear it . . .' She swallowed and looked away. 'If Kit were here he would stop it, I know he would. My father was clever, I knew there was something wrong when they sent Kit back so soon. My father knew what he was doing. There's no one now, no one.'

The desolation on her face decided him. He steeled himself to climb up the face of the house towards her. But suddenly she pushed back her hair, wiped her nose and eyes on her hands and stared down at him.

'No one, except you, Peg. You must help me.'

'Me? But what can I do?'

'You must talk to Sir Richard. I saw his face when they – they handed me over to that – that creature. I think he feels for me. I think he knows it is wrong to give me away like this, against my will, like a parcel of goods my father can sell for a good price. Sir Richard was kind to me when he was here before and I think he knows Lord – Lord Lovat . . .' and her voice withered with scorn, 'better than we do. Remember, he went to see him for my father, to arrange this – these – these *nuptials* . . .' Again her voice was scathing. 'Please, talk to him, Peg, somehow, talk to him.'

John hesitated. 'Well . . . I am to see him after the hunt tomorrow. I told you I have a message for him. I will try – I will try to tell him about you and how you feel about the wedding.'

Suddenly, Christina whirled away from him. A voice sounded inside the room and she slammed the shutters behind her. John slipped into the shadows, flattening himself against the wall as the shutters opened again and Lady Elizabeth peered out. 'Who is there?' she called. She turned back inside. 'To whom were you speaking, Christina?' he heard her say and then smiled as he heard Christina say, 'To myself . . . who else is there to speak to now that Kit's gone?' The shutters closed again but still he took care to move silently, hugging the wall, back to the kitchen.

He needn't have bothered. The celebrations, just finished up in the great hall, had hardly begun out here. The servants gorged the remains of the feast as if they had never eaten before. A new barrel had been breached and ale quite literally flowed, spilling on to the ground and splashing about their feet. The kitchen door was wide open and a mass of people ebbed and flowed in and out, capering and screeching to raucous bagpipes. John drew back but Old Nance spotted him. She held out a wooden cup, slopping ale over her bony fingers.

'Come on, my little peg-leg sprat,' she said, slurring her words and beaming, whacking her clogs down on the floor, entirely missing the beat of the music and spilling more on each stamp of her feet. 'Ye must give 'ealth to the bride . . . 'tis ill luck else.'

John felt that the ale would choke him, but if he refused they would take it amiss. It would take more than luck to make Christina into a happy bride. He squashed a sudden disloyal thought that perhaps the bridegroom might need luck too with Christina as an unwilling wife. But he took the cup and drained what little was left from running down Old Nance's scrawny arm. Luck! Perhaps he was the one who needed luck. What was he to say to Sir Richard in the morning?

Suddenly, he realized he had left his tool bag in the kitchen. How stupid could he be? He threaded through the heaving bodies, catching sight of a sudden scuffling movement in the corner beyond the fire where he slept.

William was crouched in the shadows. The slack, sly face was peering intently into the tool bag. John pushed his way over to him, tripping over arms and legs, servants flat out on the floor in the now wet, greasy rushes.

'Hey! Leave that alone. It's mine!'

He lunged for William, but too late. William turned a triumphant sneer towards him, an arm above his head.

'Ho, then, you limping gimp. Thievin' from the young mistress? Wanted something of 'ers to keep by ye, did ye?'

'No. Leave it.'

'Leave it? Leave it? What's this, then? What's this?'

And he held up Christina's clogs for all to see.

Chapter 9

Sir Basil loomed over him. They stood in the great hall, Sir Richard watching, close-eyed, from a little distance.

'In the yard, you say, boy?'

'Yes, sir.' John tried to keep his voice steady. 'They were – they were on the ground under the windows of the bedchambers, sir.'

Sir Basil turned to Sir Richard. 'She may have thrown her belongings through the window,' he said. 'With that temper it is a wonder we have anything left in the house. I have done all I can to restrain her . . .' He grinned. 'At least, thank Sweet Jesu and your good self, someone else has that thankless task now. But . . .' he shook his head and wheeled back on John, 'that doesn't explain why you have kept the clogs.'

John lowered his head, biting his lip. 'Sir, I – I . . .' He looked up squarely at Sir Basil and took a quick breath. 'I wanted to return them to he— to Mistress Christina without – without embarrassment to her.' As he spoke he knew it was a poor excuse but it was the best he could do. Sir Basil cocked an eyebrow.

'Huh! You never thought to keep them, sell them,

give them away to a sister perhaps. None of that entered your head, boy?'

'Sir . . . no, sir. They are too small for me and the patterns on them are for a girl. I couldn't wear them. I haven't any sisters and I wouldn't have sold them, sir, I give you my word.' At least all that was the truth. But Sir Basil just sniffed and frowned.

'Sir – please . . . perhaps Chr— the young mistress dropped them accidentally . . .'

Sir Basil banged the clogs down on to the table and rounded on him. 'My daughter is none of your business. Finish what you have to say to Sir Richard and be gone from my house.'

Shaken, and even more nervous of Sir Richard now, John went out into the yard. He turned to face Sir Richard who had followed him. They stood a little apart, John with his tool bag hitched over his shoulder, shifting from foot to foot, ready and more than willing to leave this trouble-filled house.

'Well, boy?'

Sir Richard's pale, blotchy face looked unhealthy and his hat covered bald patches that looked red and sore, but at least he didn't look angry. John went closer to him.

'Sir, my Master has sent me to find you.'

'And he is?' Sir Richard seemed to squint at him and John realized that his eyes had their foxy expression because he did not see well.

'The Master of the *Esperance*, sir.'

Sir Richard looked away briefly, lowering his head. He seemed to mutter something . . . a name, perhaps. He looked back at John.

'What is amiss?'

'The ship is in need of repair. She is at Highwold . . . My Master asks you to come.'

Sir Richard nodded, furrowing his close-knit brows. 'Highwold. Yes, yes. I see. What happened?'

'To the ship? We were attacked, sir. The ship is badly holed on one side but I don't know what else. The Master says he cannot leave her, not there in Highwold.' Sir Richard nodded again and John dared a little smile. 'I'm no seaman, sir, so the Master said I could be spared and he said I could be – could be trusted.'

'Sir Richard won't trust me after all that with Sir Basil,' John thought, but the man simply pursed his lips and thought for a while.

'Who attacked the *Esperance*?'

'I don't know, sir, except that it was a bigger ship, a cog they said it was, called the *Elephant*. Pirates, they said. She was burning fast when we left her.'

'The *Elephant*! Sweet Jesu!' muttered Sir Richard, looking away again. He took a few steps across the yard away from the house on his spindly legs, turned back and jerked his head for John to come to him. His arms were crossed over his narrow chest and his fingers drummed ceaselessly on his rich velvet sleeves. He glanced up at the windows and spoke in a low voice.

'Tell your Master I will do what I can. I will come to him as soon as it is possible but it may not be easy for . . . for several reasons. How long have you been waiting for me?'

'Some days, sir.'

'Then go straight back to him and—'

'Sir,' John interrupted as respectfully as he could. 'Sir, I cannot go to him directly. The Master said for you to go to him and for me to go back through Fairholm, so no one would know we had been together.'

'More and more difficult. Very well, I will – I will find means to come to him. Go on your way. Go through Fairholm as you were bid. When you get to the *Esperance*, if I am not there, tell your Master I will be with him before long. Give him my word.'

He looked away, and started to walk towards the house, his fingers still drumming. John hesitated, remembering his promise to Christina.

'Sir,' he said.

Sir Richard turned, his thin lips pursed, his face still anxious.

'There is one other thing . . .'

'Well?'

'Mistress Christina asked me to speak to you too.'

Sir Richard looked astounded. 'Mistress Christina? What about her? What can *you* possibly . . .?' He took a step closer. 'Have you not just been told that Mistress Christina is not your business?'

'Sir, Mistress Christina was in – in great distress. She – she begged me to speak to you about . . .'

'What do you mean, she begged you – when? A young woman of good family does not beg the likes of—' He cut himself off sharply and bit down on his thin lips. He looked at John and with a small shake of his head said, 'When did you speak to her? She should not – you should not . . .'

'Sir, I know, but . . . it was almost by accident.' He decided quickly to skate over the night-time meetings. 'I – she is badly upset – about the marriage that – that you – that her father has arranged. She said that you might understand and help her . . .'

Sir Richard took a step back and put a hand to his forehead, kneading a fleshy lump that looked pink and swollen. He shook his head slowly, glancing at John from the corner of his eye.

'Help her? But to do what? Everything is settled. What can I do?'

'I don't know, sir. But when I said that I was going to see you with a message – I didn't say what the message was or who from,' he said hastily, 'anyway, she asked me to tell you how she – how she felt. Sir, she was – she was very. . .' John felt himself become almost breathless at the memory of Christina's distress.

'Yes, yes, I believe I understand.' Sir Richard flicked another glance at John, full in the eyes, then looked away. 'I do understand. I do not believe that young girls should be articles of commerce, either. But Sir Basil is my cousin. There are family obligations. I am deeply indebted to him for his hospitality since my house was destroyed in the storm at Fairholm. I had little choice but to do as he asked and negotiate the marriage; after all, it is how these things are arranged as a matter of course. I think there is nothing I can do, but . . .' he cleared his throat, 'the man she is to marry – well, he is not the one I would have chosen.' He looked at John directly, anxiety in his eyes. 'You see, there is a great deal of money at stake. I certainly did not realize Christina was so – distressed or . . .'

He shook his head quickly, then shrugged his shoulders, glancing behind him. 'Listen. Be on your way to your Master and forget about all this . . .' He nodded curtly towards the house and backed away from John. 'Think no more about it. It is best left.'

He turned and shambled away towards the stair up to the great hall. He used the rail to heave himself up the first few steps, seeming heavy and cumbersome in spite of his frail-looking body. John's heart sank. Certainly this was no hero who would fly to Christina's aid and yet somehow, in spite of the way he looked, he felt he was a man to be trusted. Halfway up the stair Sir Richard leant down towards him and whispered, 'Go, boy, go. I'll do what I can. I'll do – what I can.'

John nodded his thanks, sighed and limped out through the gateway, hefting his bag on to his back. He set off across the square without looking back. He would like to have seen Christina and told her that he had done his best for her, but he could think of no way it could be done. She might come to her window that night, but he couldn't wait that long. He must get back to the Master as soon as he could. Everything seemed so muddled somehow, but at least if he got back to the *Esperance* he would have achieved one thing.

A fine drizzle was falling, but the air felt fresh and clean. John's spirits rose a little as he passed under the house gate and across the square, glad to be doing something positive at last. He went on for some way, into the woods. A squall of rain suddenly pelted down and he hurried under a sheltering tree till it should pass, wishing he had gone to say goodbye to Old Nance. She would have given him food for the journey, and now he would be back to begging once again.

The rain eased, but suddenly he heard horses coming behind him from the direction of the town. Another confrontation with Sir Basil was the last thing he wanted, so he waited, not exactly hiding in the trees, he told himself, but not showing himself on the path either.

The horses came on sedately, certainly not at Sir Basil's usual gallop, and John was about to emerge on to the path when he saw Christina on the first mount. On either side and a little behind her, rode two women. One slumped on her horse; the other sat stiff and uncomfortable, her face sour, her fingers clutching the reins. Behind them was William. The hood of Christina's velvet cape had fallen back, letting her long plait escape. William's eyes were fixed on the plait as it swung freely with the slow rhythm of her pony. John drew back into the trees and watched as the horses ambled by.

He had a sudden vivid picture of Christina astride her pony, flying over the countryside, clearing ditches at one bound. He realized for the first time what it must mean to her to be held almost a prisoner like this. How she must hate sitting so awkwardly, that great long gown dangling round her feet, the women eyeing her every move. How she must hate William watching her like a predatory animal, enjoying her discomfort – and, by the look on his face, thinking bad thoughts about her. Anger welled up but he pushed it away; it wouldn't help Christina.

The little party passed near enough for John to see her clearly. She looked straight ahead, her head high, and John could see her jaw moving as if she were clamping her teeth together tightly to stop angry tears. As she came closer he took a sharp breath. On her cheek was a livid bruise that stretched from her cheekbone to her chin.

Who had done that to her? Her father? For a moment he panicked. Was it because of something he might have said to Sir Richard about her? He prayed not. He made himself think calmly for a moment. This wasn't the ordinary beating a father gave his child. Sir Basil was an angry man, but John was sure he would never lash out at her and mark her in this way. But who else would it have been? Not her mother. An accident, perhaps . . .

The little party passed placidly, the women demure but clearly bored as they looked about them, William still watching Christina like a hawk from hooded, lustful eyes.

John reddened. William licked his lips, not taking his eyes from her. John gripped his tool bag, the blood leaving his face, finding that he was almost giddy with anger. He had a sudden satisfying picture of William on the ground, his fist burying itself hard in that soft belly again and again. He had to fight to steady himself. What was happening to him, that he felt like this? He didn't start fights, hit people in anger. That wasn't the way his father had taught him. He didn't understand. He tried to calm himself, concentrating on Christina. William could do no more than think about her, but she was helpless and unhappy in other ways, and that he did understand now. He wanted her to know he had kept his word and spoken to Sir Richard. But he wanted more. He wanted her to be free, not just of William's foul gaze but of plodding about the countryside a prisoner in her clothes, every breath she took under surveillance, given away to a man she didn't know, that terrible mark on her cheek . . .

Fists clenched in frustration, he watched the horses disappear round a bend in the path, hidden by the undergrowth. They were riding so slowly he thought they wouldn't go far before turning back. How he would manage it he didn't know, but Christina must know he had kept his promise. He moved out firmly on to the path and set off, following the riders. Sure enough, after a while he heard the jingle of harnesses returning.

Christina's eyes widened as she saw him. She gave no other sign, but reined in her horse as he went towards her.

'Peg,' she called, then, realizing her mistake, added quickly, 'Peg-leg boy! Come here!'

John felt a laugh bubbling up at the speed with which she had got herself out of an awkward moment. She frowned fleetingly and bit her lip, glancing sideways without turning her head, indicating the women who were moving up on either side of her. They stopped at a respectful distance but watched intently. John straightened his face.

'Where are you going?' she said. 'You have left our house?'

'Yes, Mistress Christina,' said John. 'I have to go back to the ship but I – I have done – what I had to do.' He looked at her hard, willing her to understand that he had spoken to Sir Richard. She gave a little nod and her face lightened.

'That is good,' she said. He let out a breath. She had understood.

'I'm on my way back to—' He stopped. Although William was still a little way behind still, John didn't want him to hear anything, especially where he was going.

'Fairholm?' Christina murmured, a question on her face. John gave a nod. He opened his mouth to try to say something more but she frowned again and gave a tiny shake of her head. She turned as William shook his reins, shoved out his chest and began to move forward as if to intervene, but the two woman waved him back. They came up on either side of Christina, glaring their disapproval, but she turned her back on them and, with a sly dig of her heel under her gown, urged her pony to dance away from them a couple of paces.

'Puddings,' she said primly, still too quietly for them to hear, and her eyes sparkled again. John almost choked in an effort not to laugh.

'Well, Peg – leg – boy,' she said, her face studiously straight, 'I wish you good fortune,' and she gave a gracious little nod of her head.

'Thank you,' said John. He bowed and stood aside to let them pass. 'Good fortune go with you . . .' he said, his face clouding over. He watched them go, the horses' gait measured and elegant, their dignified progress spoilt only by William turning back to give John two vicious fingers as they disappeared up the path.

What was to become of her? John had an uneasy feeling that simply wishing her good fortune wouldn't be enough. At least she knew he had spoken to Sir Richard, that he had kept his word. And he was oddly comforted that she knew he was going to Fairholm. It was as if there was some bond between them, though they had spoken together for so short a time and he felt sure he would never see her again. Why did that make him feel so sad? Never to see her smile again. He shook himself. Her world was not his. He had done what he could for her. He must return to the ship and the Master. The repairs would surely begin soon, and when they were done, at last his search for Aaron could go on. It was just that he wished – he wished his last picture of her was not of that awful bruise down her cheek . . .

The rain had stopped, but not, he thought, for long. He hoisted his tool bag on to his shoulder and began to hurry, dot-and-carry, down the path towards the river. He must cross it before nightfall or spend the night in the open. With a shiver, he skirted the town gibbet, blackened with damp, standing on its solitary hillock, stretching its creaking arm into the bleak rain-sodden air for a noose to hang from the groove at its end.

Suddenly he wanted more than anything to see the calm face of Brother Edmund. He would return to Fairholm and the hospital as soon as he had delivered his message to the Master. While the repairs were under way he would work with the brothers, whose world was at least familiar. He pulled off his hose and waded across the ford knee-deep, rubbed his legs dry with the cloth in his bag and turned his face to the coast.

Chapter 10

'*Esperance! Esperance*, hallo-o-o!'

At last he had reached the riverbank. John waved frantically at the ship on the far side in Highwold, jumping up and down, willing someone on board to see him. He had hoped they might even be watching out for him, but he had been gone so long now, they must have given up.

His foot gave out and he slumped down on the rickety wooden jetty, wrecked and abandoned ships on either side of him, creaking and groaning under the fast-ebbing tide. Since he couldn't swim, there was nothing to do but wait till someone saw him. But looking at the ships close to him, he noticed a few small boats and coracles tied up alongside them here and there. Further up the river, too, pulled up on to the sand, were other small craft. He had never rowed a boat on his own, but he could try.

Coracles were difficult. Jack had said they spun round like tops if you didn't know what you were doing, so he settled on a small boat that looked sound. He would ask Jack to help him return it in the morning. In the meantime, it was moored to the end of the jetty so he wouldn't need to wade out with it into deeper water before he could push off. But oars were a different matter. He searched around, even venturing into one of the dark, deserted houses at the riverside, but he found nothing. He stared down at the water swirling round the piers of the quay, dragging at them as if trying to pull them over and bear them out to sea. He shivered. He tried another yell at the *Esperance* yonder, but still no one heard him.

The river level was dropping quickly. It might soon be shallow enough for him to be able to punt himself over rather than having to row, and that he thought he might be able to manage. He searched anew, this time for a single length of timber light enough but strong enough to use as a punting pole, and came across a jagged spar dangling loose from the jetty. He ripped it away and did as best he could to hammer flat the nails sticking out from it with a mallet from the tool bag. He dropped it down into the boat he had chosen, followed it with the bag and then gingerly clambered down the cross bars of the jetty, his foot slipping on the weed that hung from them like tattered ribbons. In the shadow of the pier it was dank and ominous and the eddying water seemed blacker and deeper than it had from above.

The *Esperance* was moored downstream from him, so he hoped that the current, running strongly now down a yawning channel out in the centre, would take him towards her, so that all he would have to do would be use the spar to manoeuvre him in to her side. He stuffed the mallet into the bag, untied the rope tying the boat to the jetty and gave a gentle shove out into the murky light. He gasped as the current seized hold and swept him mid-stream before he even had time to pick up the spar. The little craft swung and rocked frantically as he tried to scramble into position. He grabbed the sides as the current grew swifter and, listing dangerously, the boat whirled faster and faster, passing the *Esperance* and heading out to sea. For a moment it looked as though they would crash into the side of the ship towering above them but they were carried past, a brush with the anchor rope setting them spinning giddily. John hung on in desperation, yelling as loudly as he could, but not daring to look up to see if anyone had noticed him.

Ahead loomed the huge sandbank that they had narrowly missed on their way in to Highwold. The channel veered round it. Somehow, he must get to it before he was swept past it out to the open sea. He scrabbled for the spar. He just might manage to steer out of the fast-running water into the shallows and wade on to the sandbank from there. He stuck the spar over the side as he had seen the Master do with the great rudder on the *Esperance*, but the current snatched the flimsy bit of wood and swept it away, leaving splinters in his hands. It tumbled over and vanished in the seething water. The boat gave a sickening lurch and keeled over. John hung on to the side, his hands sore and bleeding, but with a jolt, his tool bag shot over the edge and down into the water. With a cry, he let go, reaching out in desperation after the bag, soaking his tunic, water splashing into his eyes, coughing, choking, spitting out grainy salt water, but the bag was gone.

The boat rushed onwards, dipping and swirling, past the sandbank, heading towards the sea. There was a sudden lurch and a sheet of water washed over the side, knocking him over. His fingers scrabbled against the plank seat. It came loose and caught his chin, pushing him under, taking his breath. He clawed at the air but the little craft tilted over and more water cascaded in.

'I don't care,' thought John, suddenly too tired to struggle, 'I don't care any more ... The tools have gone, everything's gone – everything and everybody... I can't do any more. I can't. If I'm to be next ... I might as well get it over ...' Suddenly limp, he slumped over the side, his eyes closed. The icy torrent swept over his head and tugged him overboard. The little boat bobbed and bounced away from him on the tide. The water took him and flung him over, his head now clear, catching glimpses of the grey clouds overhead, now under the waves, seeing nothing but a strange welcome darkness. As the current took him, thoughts sped past him ... the roar of the scaffolding as it fell the day his father died, Hugh lying cold and white on his bier, Aaron's great black eyes full of fear as his father was led away a prisoner through the howling crowd, the huge dark echoing vault of the cathedral ... and the angel ... his father's angel ... and now his own angel ... well, there were no angels here. He let himself go, over and over in the flood, wherever it wanted to take him ...

But it wasn't that easy. Suddenly, in spite of himself, he began to fight for great gulps of air. On their own it seemed, his arms and legs began to thrash about till, after a moment or two of blind panic, his feet touched the bottom. He pushed forward into the shallows and collapsed on to his hands and knees, half crawling, half dragging himself on to the shore of the sandbank where he collapsed face down, exhausted. With his last strength, he burrowed into the damp sand, curling up, his arms twined together over his head, almost warm, almost cosy . . .

But after a while he shifted a little, the chill began to seep in and he started to shake uncontrollably, his splintered hands sore and stiffening up like his foot, his legs and arms, his body . . . He wondered how long it would be before the tide rose, and when it did, if he would be able to move or if he would drown properly this time.

'Hoi!'

John started.

'Hoi!' The voice came again.

John forced open sticky eyes and listened. Oars! Surely that was someone coming, pulling down the river with the tide. He tried a yell, but nothing came. With a huge effort, he scrambled to his knees. He peered into the mist gathering over the river, clutching his arms round his chest, shivering violently. The water in his ears was gurgling and ringing, making him deaf, but surely . . .

'Peg! Where've you got to, ye young fool?'

Hairy Jack was pulling towards him in the coracle.

He gave a hefty tug on one oar and the coracle spun round and headed in to the sandbank. He leapt out, pulled the little craft up on to the beach and plunged through the soft, sucking sand towards him. With one strong movement, he bent forward and caught John up in his arms.

'Ye young fool. Thanks be to the good God and all 'is blessed saints in heaven – I seen ye go past. What ye tryin' to do to yerself?'

'N-n-n-n-obody h-heard me, so I – I . . .'

' 'Nough o' that. Let's get ye back,' and the big sailor stumbled back across the sand, laid John in the coracle and pushed off.

'M-my father's tools . . .' said John, pleading, trying to sit up.

'Keep still. We'll fetch 'em the morrow.'

'No,' said John, sobbing, 'they're not on the sandbank, they're – they're . . .' and he jerked his head down towards the water sluicing past the coracle. Jack managed to row and shrug at the same time.

'They'm gone then, lad,' he said. ' 'Tis deep out 'ere, even at full ebb.'

'But—'

'Listen. We got *you*, thanks be to God. Tools ye can get.'

'Not those. Not my father's. They're all I had left.'

Jack shook his head. John tried to stop the tears running down his cheeks, mixing with the salt water and the drizzling rain that had started again. At the *Esperance*, eager hands reached down to haul him up the rope-ladder over the side. He was stripped and rubbed down with a rough blanket. The cook gave him a bowl of warm gruel and Jack, with a surreptitious look at the mate, loosened the tarpaulin on deck, slit open a bale of fleece, took some out and wrapped him up, warm and dry.

'Better?'

John nodded, huddled down near the cook's stove and started to pick the worst of the splinters out of his fingers. He let out a heartfelt 'ouuuch', as Jack squatted beside him, grabbed his wrist and started to help, none too gently.

'What was you tryin' to do, fer sweet Jesu's sake, Peg?'

'Ow! Jack, that hurts . . . I called and called for someone to pick me up, but no one heard, so I tried to row over . . .'

Jack laughed. 'Row? Young Peg-leg? Like to 'ave seen that, I would. Nay, nay. Should've waited, lad. We'd 'ave 'eard ye in the end.' He looked at John under bushy eyebrows. 'Where ye been, young Peg? I was worried. I even asked the Master but 'e wouldn't—'

'The Master!' John suddenly remembered why he had been in such a hurry. 'I have to see the Master,' he said, pulling his hand free, 'now, at once. I have to – I . . .'

'Master's ashore,' said Jack. 'Back on the morrow. Any road, what ye want to see 'im for?'

John went red, pulled the fleece round him tighter and said nothing. Jack raised his eyebrows but asked no more questions. It would be a relief to tell Jack, thought John, someone, anyone, to share his troubles,

118

but he had given his word. Tired out, his ears still singing with the sound of the river, he keeled over, the fleece flapping free. Jack picked him up, tucked it round him and, sneaking another look at the mate, lifted the tarpaulin and pushed John underneath, where he nestled into the open bale of fleece and slept.

He awoke in the dark. The sky had cleared and the stars shone like grains of precious salt spilt across the black sky. He thought of the glittering salt cellar on the table at Eastwych and then of Christina. What was happening to her? Whatever it was, he felt certain she was miserable and he could do nothing about it. Like Aaron and like Hugh, she was gone. But she, like Aaron, like Hugh, had mattered to him. They had all mattered to him more than he could say, but they were gone, just like his father. Suddenly, all these thoughts of pain and loss became unbearable. He must move, do something, so he didn't have to think any more. But as he started to wriggle out of the bale of fleece he remembered his clothes were still wet and that someone had taken them away to dry them. He smiled to himself. Some things did come back. No, Christina's world was not his. He hadn't belonged there and wouldn't see it again. But perhaps – perhaps Aaron *wasn't* gone for ever. He was just lost for a while, and one day he would see him again . . . he would keep trying . . . he would . . .

As he lay, eyes open, looking up at the sky, he heard footsteps coming along the quay. He squirmed on to his stomach and peered into the darkness. The stars gave enough light to see two men approaching the *Esperance*. They were walking quite freely, with no attempt at hiding. They trudged over the short gangplank and came on deck.

'This way.'

The Master led the way past the tarpaulin where John lay and up the ladder to the stern-castle. Behind him came Sir Richard Elleston, his drooping shoulders and scraggy hair sharply outlined in the starlight. John wanted to jump up and tell them he was there, but he had no clothes. And he was in among the fleece bales where he had no business to be. He stayed still, trying not to listen, but the voices carried in the night air.

'I have had many losses myself.' Sir Richard's voice was thin and reedy but clear enough. 'My old friend, I cannot do more than get you towed to the other side and help a little with repairs. I agree, it is important that the ship is repaired over on the Fairholm side instead of with these thieves in Highwold.' There was a pause as if Sir Richard suddenly realized he might be overheard. After a moment, he continued, 'But I think it impossible to give you—'

'Lend me . . .' The Master's voice was almost angry.

'Yes, yes, lend you. I would give it if I could, you know that.'

The shadow that was the Master nodded slowly.

'I will endeavour to raise the money for the whole of the repairs, but it may take a while. But for now, I have enough influence still in Fairholm to have you towed across soon.'

'Thank you, my friend, thank you,' and the Master

took Sir Richard's hand and shook it in both of his. They moved to the side of the ship and their voices became less distinct.

'Do you know who . . .'

John lost the thread but saw the Master shrug. He thought he heard the word *'Elephant'* and there was a long pause. Sir Richard came to the top of the stern-castle ladder almost directly over John's head.

'If it is who I think it is,' he said, his fingers drumming on the rail, 'then my problems are legion. There is much at stake and my loyalties are stretched.'

'Oh?'

'Sweet Jesu, the troubles we make for ourselves . . . you and I all those years ago and now . . .' He sighed and straightened up. 'But, God willing, some things we can do and the first is to get the *Esperance* to Fairholm. We must make sure there are people there still able to repair her when we find the money. My own men are dispersed but . . .'

'There are. I have sent one or two men over on the excuse that they are helping the people to clear the seaway into the river-mouth . . . an impossible task, of course, but it is a cover of sorts. They say there are many willing to work but they are almost destitute since the harbour silted up. They will need paying and we must buy materials too, of course. Their own stocks have long since been sold for bread.'

'Of course.' Sir Richard's head dropped and he sighed. 'I send them what I can,' he said, 'it is pitifully little.' He looked out towards the river. 'I should return on the tide with a tow,' he said, coming slowly down the ladder and looking up at the Master. 'Or by the evening at the latest. I won't fail you, Godfrey, trust me.'

The Master nodded his thanks and Sir Richard went to the gangplank where he turned, a puzzled frown on his thin face. His hand went up to the lump on his forehead.

'The boy,' he said.

'Boy?'

'The boy you sent to find me. What happened to him?' Sir Richard came down the ladder.

'I've not seen him. He was to come back to the Fairholm side and wait there to be picked up but . . .'

'He did not come?'

The Master shook his head.

'He was a good lad,' said Sir Richard. 'I do not think he will have run away.'

'No. He found you and gave you the message as I thought he would. There is no reason for him to run away. He wants to get to Flanders. Besides, I have something of his that he treasures. I think he would not leave, not like that.'

'Will he be safe, do you think?'

'I am uneasy. There is no reason for him to run into trouble but – where is he?'

John wanted to scramble out from the tarpaulin and show himself, but with no clothes he was too shy. He wriggled further into the bale to keep out of sight. He would get his clothes back in the morning, speak to the Master and put them out of their worry.

Chapter 11

John shivered and wrinkled his nose. His clothes were damp and smelly from drying over the cook's stove where he was cooking herring. But the herring were delicious and the clothes would dry in the wind that had got up and was blowing scuds of water across the surface of the river like strange birds taking off, landing and taking off again. Real birds were wheeling and squawking over the remains of breakfast, fighting and tearing at the skin and the bones left lying on the deck.

'Saves swabbing down after 'em,' said Hairy Jack with a grin. But the mate heard him and soon the buckets and mops were flying too.

The Master had been pleased to see John but said little about Sir Richard's visit, except that they had met and that John had done well to find him and send him to Highwold. John was on the way down the ladder from the stern-castle when the Master leant down to him and said, 'Remember, say nothing, John.' John nodded and the Master seemed to breathe a sigh of relief as if some enormous task had been accomplished.

'Oh, I have your angel, John,' he said.

John lowered his eyes and swallowed. 'I lost my tool bag in the river, sir, so I can't finish it and I – I've nowhere to keep it. Will you keep it for me till we get to Flanders?' He tried to keep his voice steady.

'Of course,' said the Master. 'I'm sorry about the tools.'

He would have gone on, but John gave a quick nod and jumped down the rest of the ladder. He rubbed his foot against his other leg with a grimace and, trying not to grieve for the bag of tools lying under the water, so near and yet so very far away, joined the energetic scrubbing-down of the *Esperance*.

Later, Jack climbed down into the coracle to cross to Fairholm.

'Can I come too, Jack?' Without tools John couldn't cut stones, but he could heft and sort them still, and at least he would see Brother Edmund again.

'Steady then,' said Jack, holding the ladder as John shinned down into the little vessel bobbing on the choppy waves. 'Want to row?' he said with a twinkle, but John settled down in the bottom and grinned.

'No, better not,' he said. 'I can row when I'm with the others in the bigger craft, but this little beast is too frisky for me,' and he patted the bottom of the coracle, feeling it stiff and brittle beneath his hand.

The 'little beast' lived up to his expectations, but Jack pulled her across the turbulent water seemingly with ease, and together they hauled her up on the beach well out of reach of the incoming tide. By now, John was anxious to see Brother Edmund and he gave Jack a run for his money up the hill. At the top, Jack left him and went down to join the townsfolk on the sand bar. John felt suddenly shy. He approached the archway into the ruined monastery and hesitated, peering round it, keeping out of sight.

The brothers were battling with the wind on the clifftop, still heaving stones, some as big as boulders that took two or three of them to shift, their long robes billowing and tangling round their legs. One of the brothers slipped and his stone rolled away, pushing him off balance. He managed not to fall, but staggered and collapsed on to a heap of rocks nearby. Forgetting his shyness, John hurried, dot-and-carry, through the archway, across the grass to the monk who lay clutching his back, his face screwed up in pain.

He arrived beside the monk at the same time as Brother Edmund. Together they helped him to his feet and, his arms round their shoulders, supported him to the hospital door where another brother took him from them and drew him inside. Through the half-open door, John saw figures in the dim light of a small fire that burned in the centre of the big room, their faces swollen and covered with red scales, some with holes where their noses had been, others lacking fingers or whole hands. They shambled along silently and stiffly, and if they caught sight of John, they turned their faces away or withdrew quickly into the shadows.

Brother Edmund looked down at him.

'Do they frighten you, my brother?'

'No ... well, perhaps. I have seen them before, lepers, but not so many together and not so ...' He passed his hand over his face and shook his head.

'They are our brothers and sisters in Christ, just as you are.'

'I know. I know they are. But they look . . . it's . . .'

Brother Edmund smiled and patted his shoulder.

'Our brothers and sisters in Christ,' he said again. 'He can see that their immortal souls are not misshapen, John.'

'Yes,' said John. He looked up at Brother Edmund, remembering cruel words once said to him about his own misshapen foot. 'So it's not because they have sinned that they are – as they are?'

'Oh, John – John!' Brother Edmund smiled. 'If sin made you crooked, we would all be doubled in two. It is a disease – that is all.'

'I knew that really,' said John, 'but someone once said my foot was – like it is – because the devil was in it . . . because I was bad.'

Brother Edmund shook his head. 'Nay, some people are very stupid.'

John smiled then looked back at the now closed door of the hospital. 'Can they be cured?'

The tall monk shook his head. 'We have no cure,' he said, 'not yet. But if God wills it, one day a cure will be found. We work for that day. In the meantime, we must care for them as we care for all God's creatures and bring them to a safe haven, especially now, when there is no money, so little help to be had. The people of Fairholm have many troubles of their own.'

John nodded. 'Hairy Jack is down there now, helping them to shift the sand from the river-mouth.'

Brother Edmund shook his head again. 'I think

only God can shift the sand, as and when he wills,' he said.

'Jack thinks so too,' said John, 'but they're his people, he says, and he can't just leave them. They need help.'

'The help they need can only come from on high.' Brother Edmund crossed himself. 'But you are right,' he said, 'willing hands and prayers will uplift their spirits and spur them on, as willing hands will help spur us on too.' Brother Edmund smiled down at John then looked around at the other monks still struggling with the stones.

'Building a new church will be almost as hard as shifting sand,' said John.

'A little more realistic, perhaps. And we have done it once before.'

John nodded.

'We learnt as we went along and we still have that knowledge. But there were masons hereabouts to help us then, when the churches were building at Eastwych and at the other towns along the coast to the north. The masons are gone now, but we will manage with the help of Christ Jesu and his saints.'

'I wish I had my tools . . .' John closed his eyes and shook his head. He explained what had happened, leaving out the way he had let himself fall into the water.

Brother Edmund frowned in sympathy, biting his lip. 'I'm sorry,' he said, 'you must be very sad to lose them. But there are always things to be done. You can help with the stones to be sure, but we have no food.'

'I've begged for food before. Do you want me to try now?'

'Will you? That would indeed be a great help to us. It is possible that a new face will bring sympathy. But I must warn you that sympathy is hard to come by in Fairholm. Do not be despondent if you return empty-handed. The people – the people are good but they are hungry too. But at least God has spared us the water in the wells. That is still sweet and not dried up, but food . . .'

John nodded. Brother Edmund gave his shoulder a pat and he turned towards a second gate in the monastery wall that led to the cluster of houses a little way back from the clifftop. Away to the left, the windmill's sails stood motionless, though the wind was still strong off the sea and the leafless trees on the cliff edge stooped over, groaning in its path. The tattered sails rattled and a strip of torn canvas slapped against the rain-blackened body of the mill. Beyond it, the remains of St John's church tower teetered on the edge of the cliff, as if wondering whether to jump and join its fellows at the bottom of the sea.

Across the green, there was no reply to his knock at the first few doors he tried, though at one house a haggard face peered through a shutter and then slammed it. Then at another, a pale, straggle-haired woman answered. Her cheeks were yellow hollows, her eyes sunk in deep sockets, the bone of her nose sharp through the skin.

Sadly, she shook her head, her voice little more than a whisper.

'We have nothing,' she said. 'My grandfather is dying and I cannot feed him. I'm sorry. Tell the brothers, I am sorry,' and she closed the door.

John was no longer sure about begging. Before when he had begged, the people had food and to spare. They had known him too. But here it was different, desperate, and he was a stranger. His last knock was much quieter, and when there was no response he tried to squash a feeling that he was glad no one else seemed to be around to ask.

A pale patch of sun picked out a rock beside the door. Wearily, he sat down on it, his head in his hands. Suddenly, he had a vision of the feasting at the great house in Eastwych. It wasn't fair. Such plenty there, such hunger here. He wondered if he dared go back to Eastwych, climb in through the kitchen shutters when it was dark . . . but would he steal? No, of course he wouldn't. But Old Nance would surely give him food for that woman and her grandfather. He looked up, almost resolved to go, but stopped. What a stupid thing that would be. How could Old Nance give him enough food for the whole village? And if he only brought a little, it would lead to quarrelling and strife, maybe bloodshed. The puzzle was too much for him. He dropped his head into his hands again.

Suddenly, the back of his neck began to prickle. Someone was watching him. He looked up. The houses were still, but a little way off he saw the figure of a boy. He stood with his back hugging the wall of a cottage at the corner of the green. After a moment, he darted forward and beckoned urgently to John.

John hesitated. Was he alone or were others lurking somewhere, waiting to give trouble? The figure beckoned again and backed away down the side of the house. John moved a little closer and stopped. There was something familiar about the boy, something he recognized . . .

He shook his head in disbelief and ran forward. Surely it was Christopher, Christina's brother. The boy had the same thick, dark hair as Christina only shorter, the same slight build – but why was he hiding like this? And why was he here, not wherever his father had sent him? And what did he want with him, John?

John paused again. Perhaps he would do better not to follow. What if Sir Basil had sent Christopher after him? What if he had discovered he had spoken with Sir Richard? Someone, William maybe, might have seen them together. What if there were people hidden, waiting to take him back to Eastwych? He edged his way to the corner of the cottage. The boy stood alone with his back to him. His head was bent over the low branch of a tree. He was picking at the twigs, throwing tiny buds to the ground and grinding them into the earth with his heel.

'Christopher?' John took a step nearer. 'Christopher?'

For a moment, the boy didn't move, then suddenly he let go the branch. It whipped back and caught him across the shoulder. He wheeled round without looking up.

'Christopher? That's your name, isn't it? I heard you called Christopher at your house.'

The boy nodded briefly, his jaw set and his hands clenched at his sides. John went even nearer.

'Are you alone?' Eyes still on the ground, the boy nodded. 'Why – why are you here? Are you looking for me?'

'It's my – my sister . . .' John had to lean forward to hear him.

'Christina?' said John and his heart seemed to lurch. 'Is she all right? Does she need help still?'

Another nod. 'She has no one else . . .'

'But you're her brother. Surely you can help her more than I can?'

'Can I? Can I, John?' The boy looked away for a moment then back, straight at him. 'Can I . . . Peg . . . ?

John stood very still, holding his breath. The eyes looking into his own were Christina's.

Chapter 12

'Christina, what – what are you doing here?'

She didn't answer, but went on looking at him steadily.

'And – oh, Christina, your hair – your beau—' He cut himself off quickly. 'Your hair – what have you done? And why are you dressed like that?'

Christina's chin went up. 'Too many questions, boy.'

She turned away, left the shadow at the side of the cottage and went over to a low wall behind it. Turning to face him, she hoisted herself on to it. Her shoulders hunched up as she supported her weight on her arms, her legs in their boy's hose dangling against the rough stone. Out here in the light, John saw the bruise down her cheek. It was fading and turning yellow and blue, but there was no mistaking it; something or someone had struck her a heavy blow right across and down her face. He had to stop himself reaching out to touch it, to smooth it away.

'Too many questions,' she said again, but dropped her head and, clasping her hands tightly in her lap, slumped forward, looking away from him.

'Peg . . . oh, Peg . . .' She glanced back at him, then

lowered her eyes. 'I needed you. You saw me with the women and this.' She felt her cheek. 'And you left. There was no one.'

John felt a rush of blood colour his face. 'Christina, I kept my promise. I saw Sir Richard. I tried to make you understand when I saw you riding out. You did understand, you did. I didn't just go and leave you; I thought it would be all right. Sir Richard said he would do – do what he could . . . I don't know what.' He shook his head quickly, his voice rising. 'But there was no use *me* going to your father. He would never have listened to me. To your brother perhaps, but not to me.'

The more he said, the more his excuses seemed to flounder, but she nodded reluctantly, and then smiled the sudden brilliant smile that dazzled him so.

'And now I *am* my brother,' she said.

John found himself blushing again. 'No,' he said, 'you may be dressed like him but . . .'

'Do I shock you again, Peg?' she said.

He paused. It was true, shocked was exactly what he was . . . shocked at seeing her again like this, shocked at the way she was dressed, her hair, at finding her alone out here in a strange place. Worst of all was the thought of what might happen to her when she was found, as she must assuredly be. He knew that now she would need someone, and he knew he would not say no.

Christina laughed at the expression on his face. 'Peg, don't look like that,' she said, 'it won't be for long. I have sent a message to my brother. He will come for me, I know, and then . . .'

133

Then, John thought, I'll be dropped when I'm no longer useful. But it made no difference, he knew he could not leave her until her brother came ... but what if the *Esperance* should be ready to sail before her brother arrived? And would he come at all?

'Who took the message to your brother?'

'Finn.'

John nodded, relieved. Finn would make sure it was delivered ... *if* Sir Basil had let him go.

'You are sure he has gone?'

'Yes ... I – I think so.'

'You don't know for certain?'

'I asked for a gift to be taken to Kit and my father agreed. He said it was too soon after Kit had gone but I persuaded him.'

No doubt she had but ... 'Did you speak to Sir Richard before you left?'

She shook her head. 'I didn't see him at all.'

'And who else knows what you have done?'

'Old Nance gave me food but that was before I cut my hair and put on Kit's clothes. She thought I was going to give it to the poor – as a kind of celebration of my betrothal.' She had the grace to look down and turn a little pink.

'That was a—'

'A lie. I know. I had to do it.'

'But why?'

She looked up, her eyes welling with tears.

'I told you ... I will never, never marry that – that creature ...'

'But he was – he didn't seem ... I mean, he looked ...'

134

'How he looked has nothing to do with it.' She was angry now, brushing away the tears, flinching a little as her knuckles brushed the bruise on her cheek. 'Why should I marry just anyone my father chooses? Why should I?' She was almost shouting.

John took a step back. 'It's all right, Christina . . . it's all right, I understand that. I do. But – but isn't that what most girls – well, girls of noble families, I suppose I mean . . . isn't what they always do?'

'They don't have to like it. They don't have to just let it happen to them, do they? *Do* they? We are not to be bought and sold like – like the oxen in my father's fields.'

'You're right, I know. I'd never thought about it before I met you because I'd never seen it happen, I suppose. Christina, I've never known anyone – a girl . . . I mean . . .'

Christina's laugh was harsh and brief. 'Like me? I'm sure not, Peg. The difference is that I will never – understand me, I will *never* let it happen to me.' She looked past him into the distance and took a deep breath. 'I have already . . .' She paused, glanced at him, then looked away. John noticed that her hands were shaking.

'You have already . . . ?' he said gently.

'You can see that I will do – whatever I have to. Look . . . I have already done it.' She brushed at her clothes and touched her hair.

Clamping her mouth shut, she slid down on the stones of the wall to stand beside John, still not looking at him. He regarded her with a worried frown. She meant what she said. Well, she was here now and would stay till Christopher arrived or . . . but the 'or' was too difficult to think about. Where was she to go?

'What are you – w-*we* – going to do?' he said.

She turned to him eagerly.

'We! You said we! I knew you would help, Peg, if only I could find you. You said you were coming here but I saw you in the distance from the woods where the little boats are carved on the trees. I saw you crossing the river with the sailor. Then later I saw you talking to the monk. You were never alone. But at last you came towards the village. It was as if Saint Christopher had sent you.'

John gave a laugh. She didn't join in, but stood with her hands together, her fingers touching her mouth. His face darkened as he saw the bruise turned towards him. He looked away to stop himself putting a hand to her cheek.

'Christina, you haven't answered my question. What are we to do? I can't take you to the ship. They'll see at once that you – well, you would have to work your passage or they won't take you and . . .'

'They'll know I'm not used to hard work, boy or not.' She shrugged. 'Peg, I don't want to go on the ship. I must stay here.'

'Here?'

'In Fairholm. I have to stay here . . . for a while at any rate.'

'Why here?'

'Because if I stay in this parish for six weeks I cannot be married against my will. Not just now to

Lord Lovat, but never. Not ever. It is the law here. Finn's Margaret, my old nurse, told me.'

'Are you sure?'

Christina nodded. 'She told me a long while ago, but I asked her again two days since and she said it was true. The women here have a choice. I'll wager they don't know how luck smiles on them.'

'So we have to hide you for six weeks? That's a long time, Christina.' He thought anxiously that the ship would surely be ready to sail long before then, but said nothing.

'You'd better call me Kit, as if I really am my brother. You thought I was him, didn't you, for a few minutes? And you know me. So people who don't will never think I'm not a boy.'

Kit. Could he manage to call her Kit? The more he thought about her as a boy the better, but it wouldn't be easy.

'K-Kit, this village is poor. No one will take you in and it wouldn't be fair to ask them. And if they find you have food they will steal it from you.'

'The Greyfriars, then?'

'Things are even worse for the brothers. They have to tend the sick. I suppose you could share your food with them but it wouldn't last much more than a day, would it, for all those people . . . ?' She shook her head. '. . . And anyway, their hospital is all that's left and it's for lepers.'

Christina recoiled with a gasp and crossed herself. 'Lepers?'

So, he thought, if the idea of lepers frightened her, she wasn't as tough as she thought she was. He hastily dismissed the memory of how he had felt when he had first seen them. But certainly the hospital was no place for her.

'Christina – Kit, where is the food Old Nance gave you?'

She nodded her head towards the trees on the clifftop beyond the village on the way to the mill. 'My horse is there,' she said. 'The food is in the saddlebags. There's water and ale too.'

'We could try the mill,' he said. 'You would at least be a bit warmer there and dry when the rain comes.'

He looked out at big black banks of cloud massing over the sea. As they hurried across the grass, John could feel the wind rising higher, gusting in spirals over the green between the little houses. Loose thatch from the roofs spun away into the air. Seabirds hovered, facing into the gale as if hanging from invisible thread. Their wide wings shone brilliant white against the steely grey of the sky, till with a screech they banked, wheeled and scudded away before the wind, like the torn sails of lost ships blown to destruction.

The coming storm seemed to bode ill. Suddenly he felt the burden of Christina and her troubles. With a flush of guilt, he wished her somewhere else – safe, to be sure, just somewhere else. He wanted to run back to the brothers or to Hairy Jack and the *Esperance*. But even there, there would be no safety, nothing really familiar and secure. When had he last felt so? He thought with a fierce longing of Aaron's little house on the hillside in the city far away. But where was Aaron now? And what was he, John, doing here with this girl who meant danger and who seemed to hold a strange menace about her, her shorn head surrounded with a halo of angry light from the fast disappearing sun.

'Will you stay with me?' Christina's voice sounded small against the rising wind but John shook his head.

'No. I will come when I can but I must go back to the ship or they will come looking for me.'

Christina glanced at him, clenching her fists. 'All right,' she said, but John could sense that she was afraid. They entered the scrubby wood at the end of the village.

'You must keep back from the cliff edge,' said John, as a sudden squall hit them and set them stumbling into the undergrowth. 'Even with the trees as shelter, the wind could have you over in no time.'

Back on the path, they found Christina's pony tethered to a tree, calmly cropping grass in the shelter of the wood. She untied him, led him towards the mill and hitched him to a post at the bottom of the rickety steps up to the door. John climbed up and pushed it open. Suddenly, the wind took it and ripped it out of his hands, slamming it. It bounced open again and keeled over drunkenly, shuddering with every blast, squeaking and groaning on one hinge.

John led the way inside. The smell of damp was overpowering and in a shaft of light from the door, he saw festoons of cobwebs mingled with huge clumps of greenish fungus clutching on to the wooden walls. The rest of the tiny room was in shadow but after a moment or two, his eyes became accustomed to the darkness. He moved forward, feeling in front of him one foot at a time. With a loud crack, a floorboard split. He jerked back just in time to stop himself dropping down to the earth below; his foot gave way and he cannoned into Christina, close behind him. Without thinking, he grabbed her hand and, to his surprise, she didn't pull it away but held on tightly.

'I – I don't think . . .' she said, and grasped his shoulder with her other hand, digging in her nails. He winced and eased her fingers away till he was holding both her hands in his own. Hers were shaking still.

'It'll be drier upstairs, I think,' he said and, bringing her with him, edged carefully towards a narrow wooden ladder that led upwards into even deeper darkness. At the foot of the ladder, he let go her hands and started to climb, leaving her at the bottom.

'I won't be long. Just hang on.'

'Peg, no! Please, don't leave me here,' she said, her eyes big with panic.

'Well, come up behind but take care.'

John reached and pushed up the trap to the next landing. Here, cracks in the shutters let in a little light. He felt his way across the uneven floor, almost tripping on a pile of sacks that sent up a shower of dust and made him sneeze. After a tussle with a rusty catch, he managed to open a shutter, pushing hard against the wind. Losing the battle, he closed it quickly and felt his way to a window on the opposite, more sheltered side. Light flooded in as he opened the shutter, showing him the huge round stone grinding-wheel in the centre of the room, reminding him of the great quern stone outside Aaron's house. A massive wooden shaft still ran up through the ceiling to the floor above but the other heavy wheels and beams lay abandoned in a heap against the wall where they had fallen.

'This is better,' said John. 'It's dry – a bit dusty, but dry.'

Christina looked uncertain. John tried again.

'At least no one will come here – and if they did, you could go up further and hide there.'

'What about my horse?'

'We can tether him below. I'll bring up the saddlebags and, look – we can heap up these sacks and you can lie on them to sleep.'

'Peg, I don't like it here. I – I . . .' He knew she meant 'I'm afraid' but could not bring herself to say it.

'What else can we do? There's no one we can leave you with. Christina – Kit, these people here are poor. You would be worth money to them. They'd guess your father would pay to get you back.'

'The Greyfriars?'

'They would *give* you back – send you back for nothing. They would think it was their duty.' He dropped his head. 'I think it may be what I should do, Christina.'

She tugged at his sleeve, panic-stricken. 'No! Don't say that. You promised, Peg, you promised.'

'But there isn't anywhere else. I can't think of

anywhere. Christina, if you went back, perhaps Sir Richard will have spoken to your father . . .'

'I will not go back. I cannot go back.'

'But Christina – Kit . . .'

'I cannot. Peg, you don't understand.'

She slumped heavily on to the pile of sacks. John crouched beside her.

'What is it, Christina? Are you so afraid of your father?'

She shook her head.

'Then what . . .?' She looked up at him and her fingers went to her cheek. 'Christina, who did that to your face?'

'He did.'

'He?'

'Lord – Lord Lovat.' She glanced away, breathing quickly, clenching and unclenching her fists.

'*He* did? But why?'

'He wanted . . . he wanted . . . he said we were as good as married and I – I wouldn't . . .' Christina's voice was flat and she stared down at the floor, not looking at him. John drew in a breath.

'So he hit you?'

'I struggled. I dug my fingers into his face. He – he ripped my gown and I pushed him away. He – he struck me with his whip.' She started to cry silently, tugging at her shorn hair with one hand, hugging her knees tightly with the other, her chin on her chest. John knew he must not touch her. He waited for a moment till she was calmer.

'Your mother, did you tell your mother?'

She shook her head. 'What could she do even if I

told her? She must do as my father says and he – he would say I must do what I'm bid by my lord. For him too, I'm as good as married. He said so before it happened. Perhaps that's why Lord Lovat thought he could . . . I didn't – I didn't want anyone to know – I was ashamed.'

'Ashamed?'

'Ashamed anyone would know I had been treated like that . . . That I was – that I was *helpless* . . . So I told them I had fallen from my horse and . . .'

'Is that why you had so many people with you, when I saw you?'

She nodded. 'I was to be taken care of, in case I fell again,' she said, bitterly. 'Taken care of . . .'

John put his hands over his face, rubbed his eyes and let his head drop into his hands. Then with a sigh he got to his feet.

'You're right, Christina. You can't go back there. But . . .'

'I'll stay here, Peg. It's all right. Come as often as you can. You'd better set the horse free or it will be seen. It will find its way home. I won't be afraid. Anything – anything is better than going back there.'

He nodded. Briefly, he put a hand on her shoulder, but she flinched and drew away. He hurried downstairs, unsaddled the pony and brought the bags upstairs. She scrambled to her feet and began to unpack them. There was bread, yellow cheese and apples, some moist ham tied in a cloth and a bag of walnuts, two pears, bruised from their journey, and a flagon of ale. Last, she pulled out a second flagon of water and put it on the floor.

'Here,' she said. 'You'd better eat something yourself.'

But he shook his head. 'I'll get food on the ship,' he said. 'You will need all this yourself.'

He went to the top of the stairs.

'I will come as often as I can,' he said gently. 'There'll be questions, Christina – Kit – but I'll find a way somehow. I won't lead them here.'

She swallowed and tried a smile, a pale echo of the dazzling smile he remembered, but enough. He turned and clattered down the stairs. Through the window he saw her watching him as he untied the horse, ran with it a little way, smacked its rump hard and sent it cantering off into the undergrowth. He turned, waved up at her and set off as fast as he could towards the town, the ghost of an idea forming in the back of his mind.

Chapter 13

As he came down the hill, John saw the *Esperance* moored safely below him at a pier on the Fairholm side of the river. Sir Richard must have kept his word and arranged for her to be towed over. Beside her were beams taken from the abandoned ships nearby that were fast breaking up. The pier was shored up with planks but looked steady enough.

John breathed a sigh of relief at the sight of the ship. No more battling with the currents in the coracle, relying on Hairy Jack to ferry him to and fro across the river from Highwold. But was Sir Richard still about? John had begun to hope that if he was told the truth about the bruise on Christina's cheek, he might come to the rescue. John felt fairly sure he was already sympathetic, but was it enough?

He stood in the shelter of one of the deserted houses on the riverbank and watched the men, busy on the ship. He saw Lou's red head leading a foraging party for more timber on the derelict ships further up the riverbank and Hairy Jack among those sawing the wood into lengths, directed by a man that John didn't know. He must be one of the Fairholm shipwrights anxious to make money at their old trade. John's spirits rose at the sight of so much activity and so many cheerful faces. There were men swarming up the mast replacing rigging and others clawing out old nails and hammering in new ones as the cut timbers were placed in position. Fleece bales lay in a great heap on the riverbank watched over by two sailors carrying pikes. It wouldn't be long before the *Esperance* was ready enough to sail at this rate. Would he have to choose between sailing with her to Flanders to find Aaron and staying with Christina?

That was a choice he didn't want to make. He looked round anxiously for Sir Richard, his confidence suddenly waning. Perhaps Sir Richard wasn't here. Perhaps he wouldn't help even if he were.

Suddenly, John heard a voice hallooing urgently. John spotted the Master looking along the riverbank towards a stranger who was cantering towards him on horseback. The man was beckoning urgently, calling out. The Master limped towards him, hurrying, and the stranger reined in as the Master neared him. They spoke together, the horseman seeming angry, jabbing his finger towards the Master who remained calm, shaking his head firmly every now and again. With a dismissive wave of his hand, the stranger wheeled and rode away, gathering speed to a gallop as he went. John ran his hobbling run down the bank to the sandy shore. At the sight of him, the Master glanced over his shoulder at the vanishing horseman, then turned back, his face darkening.

'John,' he said. 'Get on board.'

'Sir?'

'Quickly. Do as I say. You're not safe here.'

Bewildered, John opened his mouth to speak, but he met the Master's eyes and closed it again, hurried along the pier and clambered over the gunwale. The Master followed, pushing John ahead of him up the ladder to the stern-castle. He shoved him down on to a keg and stood in front of him, his legs straddled, his arms folded across his chest.

'You saw that rider?'

'Yes, sir.'

'You know what he wanted?'

'No, sir.'

'He was looking for you.'

'Me, sir?'

'Don't play the fool, boy. You'd better tell me what you have done.'

John closed his eyes and drew a deep breath. What should he say? Was this about Christina? She must have been missed by now. What else could it be? But he had promised. He wouldn't give her away. He opened his eyes and looked up at the Master's worried frown.

'I – I haven't done anything, sir. Not that I know of. At least . . . no, sir. I've done nothing.'

'Well, they are out looking for you, John. A man is dead.'

Aghast, John couldn't speak.

'The man is at Eastwych, at the house where you went to find Sir Richard for me. A man has been killed and you have been named.'

'Named?'

'As the one who killed him. A murderer, John.'

'No, sir, no. It isn't true. I couldn't kill . . .' and he remembered the fight on the ship, the chisel and the blood. He might have killed then – mightn't he? But that was in battle, not – not in cold blood.

The Master's face softened. 'Nay, John, I think you did not kill him, whoever he is, or I would not be standing here with you. I would deliver you straight as a prisoner to Eastwych. I think you do not have it in you to kill. But someone thinks you did and that will be enough. I know a little of that family. They think themselves – perhaps not above the law, but they will save their own skins if the man's death is at their door. It would be useful to have you as a scapegoat.'

He looked off into the distance in the direction the horseman had gone and then glanced round him at the busy ship, the men occupied and not noticing the two of them out of sight behind the rail of the stern-castle.

'We'll hide you here – or perhaps . . . perhaps it would be better if you took sanctuary at the church. Part of it is still standing and they cannot touch you there.'

John nodded. The church was close to the mill and Christina. But what use would that be if he could not get to her? Murder – he would be charged with murder if he were caught. Who had named him? Why should anyone think he had done such a terrible thing?

'We will wait till sundown,' said the Master. 'One of the men can take you there and see you are safe. One who can keep his mouth closed.'

'Could it be Hairy Jack, please, sir?' John's voice

trembled. The Master gave a brief smile and touched his shoulder.

'Who – who is it that's dead, sir? Do you know who it is?'

'Not his name. He was a guest at the house.'

'Not Sir Richard?'

'Nay, nay. He is staying there, but he only left us this noon when the ship was anchored. This other man was dead by then, it seems.'

With a shock, John realized it must be Lord Lovat. It must be Lord Lovat who was dead and someone thought he had killed him. He looked up, cold and shaking. The Master was going down the ladder to the deck. He opened the doors to the store under the stern-castle and moved things about, rearranging some, pulling some out on the deck. He looked up at John.

'Quickly, boy, before the crew realizes you are here. There are one or two who would hand you over if there's money on your head. Stay here until I let you out. If you hear strange sounds, voices you do not recognize, keep still . . .'

'Still as death,' thought John. As he stumbled down the ladder, he noticed the cormorant spreading its wings on the prow of a derelict ship up the river. 'I don't believe in the devil,' he said to himself, 'and omens and all those other things.' But he shivered as he bent and squeezed himself into the cupboard. The Master closed the doors, piling nets, ropes and lanterns over him, making sure he could breathe. John heard him limp away, calling for Jack as he went. He lay curled up, wedged into the tiny dark space, his foot already beginning to cramp under the weight, already beginning to sweat, already beginning to find it difficult to breathe. If they caught him, is this what it would be like in jail – black and stifling and full of searing pain? Why did they think he had killed Lord Lovat? And who had done it if he had not? Sir Basil? Hardly. He wanted Lord Lovat as a son-in-law. Sir Richard? John couldn't believe him guilty. William? William was capable of murder, he was sure, but why? He had no cause, unless Lord Lovat had seen him looking at Christina and gone for him first. Why did they think it was him, John? There must be a reason, but what it might be defeated him.

But he was innocent. They would realize they had made a mistake, they must do. And once he got to the church, he would wait till Jack had gone back to the ship and he would slip out and tell Christina it was safe to go home. There would be no marriage now. And she would tell them he hadn't killed anyone. She had seen him after he had left the house and no one was dead then. She would tell them and they would believe her . . . wouldn't they? Wouldn't they?

By the time Hairy Jack let him out, John was only semi-conscious. Jack thumped his chest, rubbed his limbs back to life and carried him down to the pier where he set him on his feet. John reeled and staggered like a baby learning to walk.

The night seemed full of noises. The boat creaked, the water lapped, a night bird called, men snored and murmured in their sleep as Jack avoided the watch and led John up the hill towards the town. They skirted the monastery wall, keeping close to it and watching carefully, often turning to look behind them. Suddenly, John tugged Jack's arm in alarm. Surely that was a movement in the trees back there? They froze, their backs against the wall, Jack muttering curses at the moon that raced fitfully across the sky between the clouds, making shadows move.

But everything was quiet and on they went, both starting at a sudden cry of pain from deep within the hospital walls as they passed. An owl swept down low, its eyes glittering in the moonlight, and somewhere far off, a dog fox barked and a vixen answered. John shivered as he became aware of a strange pulsing beat. He shook his head and gave a wry grin as he realized that it was his own heart thumping.

They neared the windmill. He looked up at the windows but nothing stirred. Would Jack want to lock him into the church tower for safety or would he manage to steal back to the mill and tell Christina everything that had happened and persuade her to go home?

A single yew tree stood at what had once been the entrance to the churchyard. Most of the wall had fallen with the rest of the church down to the beach and into the sea but a rough path still led to the tower. Trying the door, Hairy Jack offered up a little prayer of thanks to Saint Nicholas that it was open.

'You'll be all right 'ere, then?'

Jack stood in the doorway and peered into the

small room beyond. John nodded. Jack clapped a hairy hand on his shoulder.

'They can't get at you 'ere,' he said. 'You're safe so long as you do stay inside.' He paused, backed away a little and looked down at John with a puzzled frown. 'Peg . . . what is it you done? The Master never said. But it must be somethin' – For sweet Jesu's sake, lad, what you done that they're goin' to take ye an' string ye up?'

John's stomach lurched and his knees weakened. Jack's words suddenly brought home what could happen to him. He tried to blink away a sudden vision of the gibbet standing gaunt up on the hill against the sky. That was what they wanted to do to him. That was where it would happen if they caught him. He swallowed hard and tried to shake the picture out of his head but all he could see was that black wooden arm and a rope swinging, swinging . . . He turned to Jack, his eyes wide with fear, his fists clenched.

'They said – they said I murdered someone,' he said, his teeth chattering, his voice rising. 'But I didn't. I wouldn't do – do that. Not kill someone. I couldn't, Jack. I didn't, I didn't.'

He sobbed, choking on his words, till Jack put his hands on his shoulders and shook him gently, letting out a snort of laughter.

'You, lad? Kill a man? Not thee, Peg.' Jack's hands were firm and steady, and John began to calm down. Jack became serious. 'They've made some mistake . . . must 'ave. Why should they say you done it?'

John took a deep breath and moved away a little.

'I don't know. I don't understand. But I know that I didn't kill him. When I left that house at Eastwych, he was alive.'

'Who was alive?'

John shook his head. Now he realized he couldn't even be certain that it was Lord Lovat who was dead, but who else would it be?

'I think it was a man, a rich, important man that came to the house while I was there.'

Jack shook his head. ' 'Tis a mystery,' he said, 'but mark me, Peg, they'll be out lookin' for you. Don't you come out of 'ere, whatever you do. Stay 'ere – stay 'ere and may Saint Nicholas and all the saints keep ye.' He started to back away down the path as though reluctant to leave him. 'Wish I could lock you in, but there's no key. Don't you come out for anything . . . not for anything till 'tis settled and the Master sends me to get ye.'

John nodded. He turned to go into the tower. Behind him, he heard Jack's soft footsteps padding away from him. He turned back at Jack's loud whisper from under the yew tree. 'Remember . . . you don't come out of 'ere, no matter what, Peg. You 'ear me?' John nodded and raised a hand in farewell. The moon sped behind a cloud and Jack vanished into the night.

John closed the tower door but the darkness was so complete that he opened it again just a crack. Did sanctuary mean that he was safe from arrest as long as he was inside, whether the door was open or not? He wasn't sure. But he would hear their horses coming. That would give him time to shut the door, wouldn't it – if . . . He gave himself a shake and looked around.

The little room was bare. Nothing had been spared. The townsfolk had stripped it of every usable object they could find. Only the bell rope still hung from the shadows high above. He shuddered as his shoulder brushed past it and set it swinging. The floor tiles were cold and cracked, but John had no wish to sit, let alone lie down. He tried to think clearly.

He wanted her to know he hadn't deserted her but there was another reason now for trying to get to the mill to see Christina. Yes, he wanted to set her free, but now she had the power to set him free too. Christina knew for certain that he had left Eastwych before the man died. Those two women riding with her didn't know him and William – William would never speak for him. But Christina could tell whoever it was that was accusing him that he hadn't done this murder. He had left the house, she had met him, and he had not returned. If they would listen to her . . . she was his only chance. He must get to her.

He was certain that he and Jack hadn't been followed, so it would surely be safe to go as long as he was back before dawn broke and he could easily be seen. He waited, his ear to the crack in the door, listening to every sound from outside. The dog fox called again and far below, the waves pounded against the cliffs. He could feel the vibration through the floor of the tower and wondered just how safe his sanctuary might be.

'Now or never,' he muttered to himself. The door creaked as he opened it a little wider and slipped through. He paused, still listening hard, then, picking his way carefully, went down the path.

Suddenly, a heavy figure dropped from the yew tree, pinning him to the ground, half-smothering him. John threw up his arms, beating about him at the blanket over his head. A knee was pushed into his back. The man caught his arms and twisted them behind him so hard that he let out a scream of pain. The blanket was stuffed into his mouth and he choked. There was a piercing whistle and he heard horses' hooves pounding across the grass towards him. Harsh voices joked and laughed as he was hauled to his feet and bound, the rope crossing over his chest catching the blanket still blinding him. Strong arms lifted him astride a horse. He tried to wriggle himself into position on the saddle, but he knew he would fall if he couldn't hold on. A man mounted behind him. He put his arms round John, holding the reins, securing him, his grip pulling the blanket tighter over his head.

'I ca— I can't bre—'

Without a word, the man eased the blanket a little and, with a whoop, set the horse at a gallop across the grass, the other mounts following at full pelt. John heard the flap of the torn windmill sail as they passed and cursed himself for his stupidity. Christina would never know why he had left her, nor that now he needed her as much as she needed him. She would think he had deserted her. Why hadn't he listened to Jack and stayed where he was? But if he had – he wouldn't have reached her anyway. There was no answer.

His brain pounded as the horse swept on, first over grass, then through trees whose branches clawed and whipped at him as they passed. They splashed through a river, and he guessed they must be on the way to Eastwych. Soon after, slowing to a trot, he felt the jolt of cobblestones under the horse's hooves and an echo as they passed under a gateway. Clattering to a halt, the man behind him slid from the saddle and John keeled over and started to fall.

He was caught before he hit the ground and someone dumped him roughly on to his feet. The blanket was tugged from his head but his arms were left roped together. He blinked. He was in the yard of Sir Basil's house, surrounded by a group of the servants he had lived among not so long ago, some of them holding knives and sticks. Why? He could go nowhere, his hands tied as they were, feeling sick and dizzy, his clothes torn from the ride through the wood. Someone shoved him against the stable wall as the horses were led away and a huge man stood guard over him, pressing him against the stones with a heavy fist, the other hand gripping a massive cudgel. Servants came hurrying from the kitchens, pushing their arms into jackets, pulling on bonnets, jabbering with excitement. At the head of them, his face on fire with glee, was William, a torch flaming above his head. He stopped in front of John and thrust the torch close to his face.

'Aye,' said William, gabbling to get his words out quick enough. 'That's 'im. That's the one. 'E stuck

156

the knife in Lord Lovat and ran off. I seen 'im with me own eyes, I did. Peg-leg John's 'is name, the filthy gimp. Murderin' bastard!'

'Close yer mouth, William.' Old Nance was bringing up the rear, shuffling along on her skinny legs. 'What d'you know about it any'ow?'

William kept on jabbing a finger at John, drawing rasping breaths, dribbling as his fat lips parted ready to start again. But before he could speak, a commanding voice came from the entrance gate.

'Take him to the town jail and make sure he's secure. There must be no accidents or escape.'

A thickset man with grey hair hurried towards them, gathering a cloak round his nightgown, his bare feet and legs shoved into boots. All heads turned towards him and the little crowd drew back from John, still held against the wall. Odd though the man looked, no one, not even William, said any more.

'Take him to the jail,' said the man again. He looked John up and down by the light of the torch, then turned to William and said sharply, 'You are a witness to this murder?' William bowed, managing to look eager and grovelling at the same time.

'No! It's a lie!' John shook his head violently, tugging at the rope binding him.

The man turned to him. 'Be quiet,' he said, curtly. 'I am the bailiff, boy. You are in my charge. You will be questioned in the morning.' He turned back to William. 'You will present your evidence then and until then, hold your tongue.' He gave a quick glance at the servants who were still gaping at the spectacle of John, the guards, William and himself all lit by the flickering torchlight. 'Get to your beds,' he said, barely raising his voice. 'Go on, be off with you.'

With scarcely a murmur, the crowd began to disperse, but as two guards grasped his arms ready to march him through the gate, John heard William's screech of triumphant laughter. It wasn't much comfort to see Old Nance cuff William's ear and snatch the torch from him to lead the way back to the servants' quarters. William lumbered along beside her, holding his head, complaining all the way. The bailiff watched them for a moment then turned to the guards.

'Has Sir Basil been told of the arrest?' The men looked at each other blankly and the bailiff gave a quick, impatient sigh. 'He would be here if he had been told,' he said. 'He must be still abed. Well, the morning will do. We have the prisoner, that's the main thing. Take him away.'

Two men began to push John towards the gate. One gripped his arm so tightly his hand began to turn numb, and with every other step he seemed to stumble and cannon into his captors or into the wall. But he was unaware of everything except the thought of Sir Basil. He would see Sir Basil in the morning and Sir Basil would ask about Christina. Why, oh why hadn't he managed to see her before he was caught? But his promise still held. He wouldn't give her away. He wouldn't. And yet – if he was asked directly, 'Where is my daughter?' what would he do? What should he do? Would he lie and keep her secret? Or would he tell the truth and so betray her?

These questions were still running unanswered through his head when the heavy nailed doors of the town jail loomed up before him.

Chapter 14

The jail was dark, stinking and verminous. Water dripped down the wall from a barred window high above his head and John huddled into a pile of filthy straw in a corner, chained by the ankle to an iron hoop let into the wall. He pulled his knees up as far as he could under his tunic to keep his feet from the cold, damp floor and the scuttling rats that eyed him with greedy, glittering eyes.

But the jailer had at least given him something to eat. The dry bread had a film of grey mould but he managed to scrape most of it off. The water seemed clean enough and the old man had refilled the cup from a bucket and left it with him. He had stood in the doorway scratching his greasy head with black nails, grumbling about the world while John ate. Thankfully, the only questions he asked were John's name, how old he was and where he lived. The last was difficult to answer. John thought it best not to mention the *Esperance*, so he gave the name of the city he had left all those weeks ago, and had a sudden vivid memory of Aaron's father being dragged off to a jail that must have been far, far worse than this.

At last the jailer gave up and shambled off. Alone,

John could worry and fret about what to do. He could only tell the truth and pray that he would be believed, but Christina was alone in the mill, afraid to stay in the dark but afraid to come out, waiting for him and not knowing where he was. Perhaps the worst thought of all was that she would think he had deserted her.

A sudden noise outside brought the moment he had been dreading. Several loud voices hailed the jailer, then one voice spoke his name but the door between them muffled it. Sir Basil? He couldn't tell, but who else would it be? A key grated in the lock and the door lurched open. The jailer manacled his hands, released his leg-iron and led him, limping, into the dreary room beyond the cell.

John gave a gasp of relief. Sir Richard Elleston was sitting at a table, his head in his hands. The bailiff was with him but Sir Basil wasn't there. Standing behind Sir Richard were two or three men John didn't know. They looked like servants, but not anyone from Sir Basil's house that he could remember. Sir Richard looked at him seriously but, John thought, not unkindly. He looked thinner than ever, and grey about the eyes. He sat up with a sigh, linking his hands on the table before him, but every now and then putting a finger to the strange lump on his forehead.

'Now, John,' he said. 'You know why you are here. Lord Lovat is dead and one of Sir Basil's servants—'

'Sir! I—'

'Do not interrupt me, John. You will have a chance to speak, but for the moment be quiet.'

John dropped his head and bit his lip, breathing quickly. Sir Richard must be made to understand that William was lying . . .

'John? Are you listening to me?'

'Sir . . .' He lifted his head.

'Very well. The charge against is that you stabbed Lord Lovat to death and then ran away. This servant is willing to swear on oath that this is what he saw. John, we are going to try you very soon. Sir Basil wishes the matter dealt with as soon as possible. I am a magistrate and am empowered to hear the trial. I have – I have persuaded Sir Basil that I should hear the evidence rather than him. He is, as you can imagine, very distressed and so perhaps, er – perhaps not able to be as – impartial . . .' He cleared his throat. 'This matter does concern his family very closely.'

John's spirits rose. He might not even see Sir Basil.

'I – I'm grateful, sir,' he said. 'When will it be?'

'Tomorrow.' John blinked. 'It is best done quickly, John. You will be taken to the court at Highwold where men that are open-minded and fair will be gathered to hear the evidence. I tried to have the trial moved to Fairholm but . . . at least Highwold is a little way from Eastwych and the murder. And you should still have a little time to marshal your – your defence.'

'My defence? But, sir, I know nothing about the murder. How did it happen? When am I supposed to have done it? What weapon am I supposed to have used?'

'Hush, John. I do not know. That is for William to

162

tell us.' Sir Richard's hand went up to the lump on his forehead.

'I didn't do it – I didn't . . . please, Sir Richard . . .'

'John, be calm.' John dropped his head. 'If you are innocent – and I bel—' He cut off quickly and cleared his throat again. 'If you are innocent, as you say, then you will be found not guilty at your trial and allowed to go free. That is justice. There is not long to wait and I will continue to see that you are cared for as well – as well as I can.'

So Sir Richard had known he was here and made sure he was at least fed and not beaten or tortured. John raised his eyes to his and gave a small nod of thanks.

'Is there anyone who will speak for you?'

'Speak?'

'Give you a good character . . . give account of your whereabouts over the last two days?'

'Only Christina,' thought John bitterly, 'and I must not, will not name her.' He racked his brains. Brother Edmund did not know him well enough. Who would listen to Hairy Jack? But then a thought struck him.

'Sir, do you suppose the Master would speak for me?'

Sir Richard shook his head slowly, considering the idea. 'Have you been on the *Esperance* long?'

'No, sir, but the Master trusted me enough to send me to you, and . . .' He thought of the stone angel still on board the ship.

'John, the trial is in Highwold and the Master – well, things are difficult for him at Highwold. More difficult than you know. To be honest, I am not sure how his word would be received there. It might do more harm than good for him to speak for you. But I will ask him what he thinks.'

'Thank you, sir.'

'Till tomorrow then, John,' said Sir Richard. He stood up, squinting up his eyes as if against a bright light, though the windows were small and the room was dim. With a curt gesture, he told the jailer to take John away. At the cell door, John turned. Sir Richard was standing at the far door, the bailiff holding it open.

'Sir Richard . . .'

'Well?'

'Er . . .'

'What is it, boy?'

'Sir – Mistress Christina . . .'

'What about her?' Sir Richard frowned and gave a quick glance through the open door. 'There is no question of marriage now, of course.'

'But . . .'

Sir Richard took a step towards him and lowered his voice. 'John, there are things more important to you now. Mistress Christina's problems are over, for the moment at least. I have not seen her. She keeps to her room in mourning, as is fitting. Her mother and father are distraught that this should have happened. Lord Lovat's family will demand retribution, no doubt. I believe his brother is already on the way to Eastwych. For the moment, finding the culprit is the main thing.'

'It isn't me,' said John, firmly.

Sir Richard slowly lifted his hands palms outwards

towards him. 'God be with you,' he said, nodded and left the room. As the door closed behind him, John thought he heard a raised voice from beyond it. He was bundled back into the cell, secured to the wall and his wrist cuffs removed, his mind in turmoil.

Was Christina really at home? Had she heard about the murder and gone back? Perhaps Finn had found her. And yet Sir Richard hadn't seen her . . .

The night passed slowly. John tossed and turned, itching from the fleas in the straw, kicking out as best he could at the rats that came sniffing about for the crumbs from the evening lump of bread he had hardly managed to eat. The jailer looked in on him once or twice and he pretended to be sound asleep. Listening to the old man's mumbling was more than he could bear.

Dawn came and the jailer gave John more bread and water and brushed off the stray bits of straw sticking to his tunic. He let John wash his face in the bucket and even gave him a rag to dry himself. Manacled, he was bundled up on to a horse in front of a burly guard, two others mounted on either side of them. The bailiff arrived and they set off at a gallop, so fast that John put out of his head any thought of rolling off and running away. As they rode up the hill the sun burst through a cloud and silhouetted the stark shape of the gibbet on the skyline. John drew in a sharp breath and snapped his head away, almost falling. The guard grabbed him tightly and they thundered on.

At Highwold the horses were taken away and men with pikes surrounded John. The bailiff went ahead as they led him stumbling across a narrow street, his wrists still manacled, hobbling along with the weight of iron on his bad foot. They passed a half-finished stone building, brilliant white in the early spring sun, still shored up with scaffolding. Builders, carpenters and apprentices swarmed about it wielding tools, hods of small stones and mortar, lengths of wood. Two worked a pulley, heaving up heavier stones to the top of the building where the roof timbers were already in place. Work stopped and fifty pairs of eyes looked down at John. Men and apprentices leant down to watch his painful progress, as he clanked, dot-and-carry, underneath the lattice of wooden poles. Suddenly there was a clatter and a ringing of metal on metal. They were cheering him on, clanging their tools together in a noisy rhythm.

'Nay, lad! Courage! Sweet Jesu save ye!'

'Blessed Saint Joseph watch over ye.' That was a carpenter. Then a builder called 'Saint Barbara keep ye, lad. Blessed Saint Barbara,' and others joined in, 'We're prayin' for you, lad ... the Four Crowned Martyrs preserve you!'

Surprised, he looked up at them and managed a shaky grin. The pikemen hustled him along to a low timbered hall that had seen better days, soon to be replaced by the grand new building going up on prosperity gained at the expense of Fairholm. The cheering rose in pitch as John disappeared inside. He was puzzled. They did not know him. He was not from Highwold. He did not see the pity in their eyes for his youth, his torn clothes, or the chains that loaded him down. The guards turned, shook their fists and swore at the workmen, then slammed the double doors on the din.

Inside the gloomy hall, John's brief moment of cheer melted away. A bald man in a long black robe sat at one end of a long table, an inkhorn, quill and parchments in front of him. The bailiff waited behind a large, imposing chair, and behind him a moth-eaten curtain hung in holes. Two rows of benches were ranged along one side of the table. John stood shivering a little, only partly from cold, still seeing the gibbet in his mind. Surely Sir Richard wouldn't let it happen . . .

The door opened. A group of men processed in and lined up along the benches, standing stiffly, their faces serious. The bailiff stood to attention. A moment later, Sir Basil swept in alone and the door closed behind him. There was no Sir Richard and no Master of the *Esperance*.

John's eyes widened and his stomach seemed to drop from his body. Only the heavy chains stopped him putting his arms across his face. Hurriedly, he controlled himself, gripping his hands together so tightly the manacles dug into his wrists. Sir Basil took his time to settle in the great chair and then looked up at John. John drew back at the venom in his eyes. He had been prepared for difficult questions about Christina when they met, but not this hatred. What kind of justice was he to expect from this man? And where was Sir Richard?

'In the absence of Sir Richard Elleston, I am your judge. Sir Richard has been – has been – taken very sick.' He glanced at John then looked away. 'These men here are to decide on your fate – if,' he added hastily, 'if you are found guilty. Let us begin.' He gathered himself, looked round him and nodded to the bald clerk who picked up his quill. 'Lord Lovat of Kersley was brutally done to death two days ago. John of Fairholm . . .'

At the name Fairholm, there was a stir among the men on the benches. The faces of the Highwold men looked at him and darkened. John opened his mouth to protest that he was not of Fairholm but Sir Basil's voice overrode him.

'You are accused of the murder. What have you to say?'

John swallowed. Two days ago? That was when he was on the way back to Fairholm from Eastwych. He shook his head. Everything was happening so quickly.

'I – I . . .'

'Did you or did you not kill the man?'

'No, sir. No, I did not.'

Sir Basil chewed the inside of his cheek and shrugged. The quill scratched slowly over a parchment and the faces on the benches remained unyielding.

'We'll see. Where is the witness?'

A door opened once more and William was pushed forward by a pikeman, his hand tightly gripping his arm. Sweat ran down the fleshy face and John could smell the fear in him from where he stood across the room. He stared at him, daring him with a look to meet his eyes, but William turned his head this way and that, avoiding him. Sir Basil cleared his throat.

William looked at him, smeared his hand across his nose and dared a glance at John, his eyelids fluttering.

'Now. You are William, my servant at Eastwych.'

William could do nothing but nod and fidget, his eyes now anywhere but on John.

'Speak up.'

'Yes sir. I am – I am your . . .' His voice gave out and Sir Basil sighed impatiently.

'You have given a deposition, taking an oath to tell the truth. You witnessed the killing of Lord Lovat.'

William nodded again.

'You must tell us what you know. Speak up, man.'

But William seemed incapable of speech and, irritated, Sir Basil snatched another parchment from the table in front of the clerk and began to ease William's passage with questions taken from it.

'This is your deposition. It is signed with your mark as the truth?' Another nod. Another squirm. 'You say here that you saw the prisoner kill Lord Lovat.'

'I – I d-d-did.'

'You say that it was late in the afternoon, after the prisoner had left my house. You had gone riding in attendance on . . . on Mistress Christina and her women. You saw him come from the woods to approach – *approach my daughter* . . . and – and have *conversation with her*.'

He could hardly choke out the words. He glared across at John, quivering with rage.

So that was it. Not only was John supposed to have killed a man but he had dared to speak to Sir Basil's daughter and it seemed that that was almost a worse crime. Christina's reputation was more precious than a man's life. William made it sound as if John had been hiding in the woods waiting to see Christina but it hadn't been like that. It was by chance. They were out in the open. There had been nothing wrong in the way they had spoken. William was lying about that as well as everything else. But William suddenly seemed to leap into life.

' 'E did, sir . . . I seen 'im. He come out and took 'er 'orse by the rein, sir, and pulled 'er to one side to 'ave private speech with 'er.'

'No sir, I didn't . . . I didn't. I did speak to her but I didn't—'

'Be quiet!' Sir Basil's snarl cut across John's eager denial. 'You will speak when I say you may speak and not before.'

John subsided, his face red with rage and frustration.

'Did you hear what the prisoner said to – to my daughter?'

William shook his head. 'Too far away I was, sir. I never 'eard nothin'. They 'ad their 'eads full close together like. Full close.'

He snatched a sly glance at John, but Sir Basil did not notice. He had closed his eyes, clenched his fists and taken a deep breath, his nostrils flaring. After a moment, he recovered himself and turned back to William.

'And then?'

'We rode back to the 'ouse, sir. I took the 'orses back to the stable and Mistress Christina, she went inside with her ladies. I tended the 'orses like I always does and – and . . .'

'Yes, yes. Get on with it, man.'

'A while later, I 'eared Lord Lovat at the top of the stair. 'E were talkin' to someone – I ain't sure who but I think 'twere Mistress Christina. Any road, 'twere a lady. Whoever it were – she went back inside and Lord Lovat started down the stair. There were a shout and a bit of a scuffle. I looked out and I seen – I seen – 'im . . .' and he jerked his head at John without looking at him, 'I seen 'im run down the stair and out through the gate as if the devil was after 'im.' He crossed himself and licked his lips. 'I runned out and I seen . . . I seen his lordship lyin' there on the ground, all covered in blood.' He started to wring his hands, a sanctimonious look on his face. ' 'Twas a terrible, terrible sight, sir, one I don't never wish to see again in all my life . . . I telled 'em to sound the alarm at once, sir, and – and the rest you do know.'

John stared across at William in disbelief. All those lies for a burnt shirt and a bare arse. Or was it jealousy because he had spoken to Christina and she would never have let William get so near? He shook his head. It made no difference now.

'It's not true,' he breathed, 'it isn't . . . it isn't . . .'

Sir Basil did not hear him but nodded slowly. 'Yes. The rest I know,' he said. He turned to John. 'What have you to say?'

'Sir, I . . .' John tried to gather his wits together. He looked at William, who looked back, a triumphant sneer in his eyes. John took a breath and straightened himself up, clenching his fists before him.

'Sir, why should I kill Lord Lovat? I didn't know him. I never even spoke to him.'

Sir Basil gave a curt nod to William.

'I did often hear the peg-leg say 'e had a fancy for Mistress Christina,' he said. 'I told 'im over and over it weren't fittin' but 'e – well, I dunno what 'e did think, but I reckon 'e thought 'e 'ad a chance with 'er. He'd got 'er clogs in 'is bag, didn't 'e . . . ?'

'Most certainly he did,' said Sir Basil, his voice tight with rage. 'I was not satisfied with his explanation then, and even less so now.'

'Sir . . .' Sir Basil's head whipped round. John tried to keep his voice calm, but his fingers were twisting together till they hurt. 'Sir, may I ask, please . . . what weapon I am supposed to have used?'

'William?'

'Oh, sir, it was one of 'is own tools what 'e kept in 'is bag. Never left 'im, that bag. It was a sharp chisel. He took it with 'im when 'e run off. I seen it. Bag over 'is shoulder, chisel in 'is 'and, the good gentleman's blood still on it.'

'No, sir! That's not true. I didn't kill Lord Lovat. I didn't run away. I didn't . . .'

'Where are your tools now?'

John closed his eyes. He knew this would go against him.

'They – they are at the bottom of the river, sir.'

'And why should they be at the bottom of the river?'

'Sir, I – I lost them overboard when . . .'

'How convenient.' Heads wagged wisely along the benches. 'I think it more likely that you threw them there so they would not be found. You thought no one would know you had such a weapon.'

'No, sir! No. L-l-losing them was an accident. I would never have thrown my father's tools away, never. I'd never have used them for killing someone either. And, sir, I didn't come back to Eastwych after I saw her – I mean, Mistress Christina. I went on to Fairholm. I wanted to reach my ship – the *Esperance . . .*'

There was an angry muttering from the benches. He glanced at faces turned to granite at the sound of the name of the ship that had escaped across the river to be repaired at Fairholm. That was a bad mistake. He should not have named her. He swallowed, suddenly overcome with desperation. Now he knew there was nothing, nothing he could say that would convince these people.

'You do not deny you waited in the woods for my daughter?'

'Sir, I didn't wait for her. It was by chance as I was leaving the house that she came by.'

'Again – how convenient. But you spoke to her?'

John nodded. He would not say she had called him to her, had spoken to him first. Blaming Christina would damn him even more.

The voice, icy with sarcasm, went on. 'And just why – why did you have the – the insolence – to speak to her?'

There was a long pause. What could he say? Even now he would not give her away. And if he told the truth about her desperation at her marriage, they would still think he had killed Lord Lovat for her sake. Christina could never speak for him now. The Master had not come. Brother Edmund had only seen him for a few minutes that day and could not vouch for him. Hairy Jack had not seen him lose the tool bag, only taken his word that it had been washed overboard. And neither could he say what he had been doing for the time he was absent from the *Esperance*, for that involved Christina. He had to say something but they wouldn't believe the truth. He lowered his eyes.

'Sir . . . she had – she had been kind to me. I wished to thank her and say goodbye.'

'*Kind* to you?'

'She – she understood about – about my foot.'

He made a half-hearted gesture towards the foot in its iron bracelet. Sir Basil gave an ironic sigh, raising his eyes then looking across at the men on the benches.

'I think we need continue this comedy no further,' he said. 'Are we all agreed, sirs?'

Every head nodded. William's eyes gleamed and his fat lips parted in a jubilant smile. John looked around for a friendly face, but knew there was none. He was alone.

Sir Basil made to rise and the bailiff hurried forward to pull back his chair. Sir Basil drew himself up to his full height. He gestured to the men on the benches and they scrambled to their feet. Twelve hostile pairs of eyes turned slowly and fixed on John like the unwinking eyes of the cormorant he had seen spreading its wings on the river. Sir Basil threw his cloak over his shoulder and, gazing over their heads, spoke slowly and with muted fury.

'John of Fairholm,' he said, 'the court finds you

guilty. Guilty of murder. Guilty – as – sin.' On the word 'sin' he snapped his head round to John. 'You hang tomorrow – *boy*.' He paused, chewed on his cheek and looked away again. 'May God have mercy on your soul, John of Fairholm, may God have mercy...'

Nonchalantly, almost as if the trial had never happened, he crossed himself. There was a scrabbling along the benches as the men followed suit. The bailiff held open the door.

'We need not trouble you any longer, sirs,' said Sir Basil with a satisfied nod to the lines of men. He went to the door, turned and with a sudden vicious sneer said, 'Aye. May God have mercy... but I doubt he will.'

Without a backward glance Sir Basil swept out and the bailiff followed him. John turned cold and the world seemed to spin. The pikeman grabbed his arm, jerked him upright and dragged him away.

Chapter 15

John was taken back to the cell in Eastwych. It was nearer to the place of execution than Highwold and the workmen on the scaffolding had looked as if they might make trouble when they learnt the verdict. They hammered on the scaffolding, bawling and jeering at the guards as John was led away.

The jailer was almost kindly when he arrived. He gave him a bowl of broth that he couldn't eat and part of an old comb for his dishevelled hair that he didn't use. Leaving his hands free, the old man only chained John by the ankle, his foot chafing and throbbing at the weight of the chain.

John's thoughts lurched and whirled till he was exhausted but still he couldn't sleep. William had lied, Sir Basil hadn't even pretended to listen, Sir Richard was sick, the Master hadn't come, but none of it made any difference. He would never know what had happened to Christina. And Aaron – he would never find Aaron now and Aaron would never know how he had tried to find him. Maybe he had tried too hard. Better he had stayed in the city, in the choir school, and never left at all.

He crouched in a corner with his head bent, his

arms round his knees, his eyes dry, his throat tight, his head throbbing. Once he had believed that, in a kind of miracle, the stone angel in the cathedral had brought him to safety out of the dark. He wished he had his own angel with him now, but no angel could lead him from this dark place. There was no way out. He was to die tomorrow.

He looked at the sky through the bars of a slit in the wall high above. Was it true? Would he see his father when – when it was over? Was Hugh up there somewhere, beyond the stars, waiting for him, perhaps? But it was the way he must follow to reach them – hanging there in the cold dawn, the ravens waiting – that made him close his eyes, rigid with fear and misery.

Hugh had died young too. He had been murdered, like John was going to be murdered. For that's what it was. John rolled over and sat up, suddenly angry. The trial hadn't been fair. He was to be killed because of William's hatred and Sir Basil's hurt pride. He was innocent, but Sir Basil didn't care and William was – well, William wasn't worth thinking about. Who *had* killed Lord Lovat? Who could have done it? And why?

And Christina? He struggled to his feet. He wanted to pace about the room but the chain held him back. She was still alone out there, not knowing what had happened. Yet supposing she wasn't? Supposing she was at home by now, just glad not to be marrying Lord Lovat and not caring about – about tomorrow. He rubbed his face with his hands and slumped down again in the straw. None of this was Christina's fault. If he hadn't met her, he wouldn't be here, it was true, but he had made the choice to be her friend. He had chosen and it had led him here, to this dingy cell and – and tomorrow.

At midnight, a priest arrived. He was short and stout, his eyes crusted and squinting as if just out of his bed. John was surprised and for a moment allowed a hope that perhaps Christina was indeed at home and that it was she who had sent him, but no.

'My Lady Elizabeth has sent me to you for the good of your immortal soul. In Christian duty and charity she has sent me,' said the priest. He raised his eyes piously to the ceiling, fell to his knees and started to preach about hellfire.

John didn't listen. Others had preached hellfire before. It had puzzled him then and it puzzled him now. What had that to do with a God that was supposed to love you? The priest offered to hear his confession, but John shook his head. He would say his own prayers. Ask his own forgiveness. But he did wish he had his angel with him.

Suddenly the cell door opened again. John looked up. From the shadows a pair of grey eyes looked down on him. John struggled to his feet. Brother Edmund. Brother Edmund had come to him. Without warning, his eyes stung with tears. He tried to speak, to tell him . . . but nothing would come. He blinked, biting down hard on a grimy fist. Silently, the tall monk came into the room and the priest lumbered to his feet and backed away.

'My brother in Christ,' said Brother Edmund, holding out his hands to John. John made to dart towards him but the chain pulled him up short and he hit the wall. In two strides, Brother Edmund crossed the cell, folded his arms around him and held him close. Then he steadied him to the ground and sat beside him in the filthy straw, keeping hold of both his hands. Watching them, the priest gave a hasty blessing into the air and, dithering with relief, sought the door.

'You will go with him to the – the, er . . .' he said, hardly bothering to turn his head.

'Yes. I will go with him,' said Brother Edmund, and the priest scurried away.

'I'm glad he's gone,' whispered John.

Brother Edmund smiled but said nothing.

'How did you know I was here?'

'Sir Richard told me,' said the monk.

'Sir Richard? But . . .'

'He is in the hospital.'

'The hospital? You mean . . . a leper?'

'We are not certain. But it was thought – it was considered wise to take precautions. He has a strange mark on his forehead. I – we do not think that it is leprosy and we have not put him with the other patients because we cannot be sure.'

'I saw him yesterday. He was to hear my trial. He seemed – perhaps not well, but not like those others I saw . . .'

Brother Edmund looked down for a moment. 'I believe,' he said, 'I believe it was Sir Basil who felt it best to send him to us. There might have been infection. He has his household to think of.'

'I see,' said John. So Sir Basil had got rid of Sir

Richard. He must have wanted to hear the trial himself very much to force Sir Richard into a leper hospital. Was this really just about John daring to speak to Christina? Perhaps he knew everything Christina had done, climbing out of the house at night, riding in boys' clothes alone, running away, and was blaming him for that? John shook his head. He didn't understand any of it.

'John,' said Brother Edmund. He smiled, then, 'Peg,' he said. 'Peg, it is useless to waste this little time in wondering. What is sure is that today you will be . . .'

'With my father in heaven?' said John, his head lowered. 'Is that so sure?'

Brother Edmund nodded. 'Quite sure,' he said. 'I believe it is quite sure.' His face lit up. 'And all his saints and angels . . .'

'I meant my own father,' said John.

Brother Edmund looked down at him a little taken aback. Then he smiled again. 'Oh yes,' he said, 'your own father too. There will be rejoicing.'

'And my friend, Hugh, that was killed?'

'Yes, Peg. I believe they are there and are waiting to welcome you.'

There was silence for a while. John seemed almost to doze, his head drooping heavily, beginning to lean on the tall monk's shoulder. Suddenly he started awake.

'Brother Edmund, please will you do something for me?'

'If I can.'

'There is a girl – her name is Christina and she

lives at – at the great house in Eastwych. I can't explain, but she is hidden. She is waiting for me, waiting for me to help her. She has run away.'

'If she has done wrong, my brother, I cannot help.'

'No, no. She was to marry Lord Lovat, the man I am supposed to have killed. She ran away but now she could go home, but there is no one to tell her he is dead. She's alone out there. Please . . .'

'I see. Where is she?'

'In the old mill not far from the hospital.'

Brother Edmund stirred uneasily. 'It is not safe there, Peg. It could fall at any moment if the weather turns.'

'Then please will you go . . .'

'I will go tomorrow, when . . .'

'When I am dead?'

'When you are with God.'

'Will you promise?'

'I promise. Now, Peg, could you say some prayers with me? I believe it will be a comfort.'

John nodded and allowed himself to lean against the spare figure sitting beside him as he started to pray. He listened to the words without joining in, letting his thoughts wander. Perhaps – perhaps what was to happen tomorrow would be easier than living, and he remembered how he had felt when he let the river take him. Perhaps it would have been better if Hairy Jack had left him there instead of saving him for the gallows.

When the jailer opened the cell door, John was asleep against Brother Edmund's shoulder and had to be roused. He opened his eyes with a gasp, then sat for a moment wishing that it was over, that he had died in his sleep without waking to face the morning. Brother Edmund helped the jailer get him to his feet. To John's relief, his hands were not manacled but tied in front of him with heavy cord.

As they passed the house, John glanced up at the window from where Christina had once climbed down to him. But the shutters were closed and the house in darkness. Was Sir Basil sleeping easily in there? Was William snoring in his bed or was he watching from somewhere, licking his lips, drooling, rubbing his hands in glee at the thought of John hanging from a rope? John looked away quickly, almost glad of the jerk of the cord that tied him to a guard. The small procession – John, Brother Edmund and three guards – went out under the town gate. Suddenly, a figure detached itself from the shadows cast by the moon. John drew back, prepared for William and anything he might do, but it was Old Nance who came shuffling out towards them.

'Peg, lad,' she said, her voice little more than a croak, 'Peg – I tried to tell 'em that you never done it but they wouldn't listen. But I tried, lad, I tried.' John nodded. He couldn't speak. He reached to take her outstretched hand but a guard put a pike to her chest and pushed her away. Brother Edmund laid a hand on the man's arm but he shrugged him off roughly. The old woman steadied herself against a wall, the wind beginning to snatch at her grubby skirts and her thin, wispy hair.

'God's blessing be with you,' said Brother Edmund. She crossed herself and watched them till they disappeared, tears running down her shrunken cheeks.

The guards were getting anxious, swearing and pulling on the rope, making John hurry. He stumbled and almost fell and they jabbed at his legs with their pikes. Brother Edmund tried to fend them off and a guard pushed between them, elbowing them apart.

'Are you not ashamed?' said Brother Edmund. 'He is no more than a lad.'

The man looked sheepish and muttered that he didn't like it either, he just wanted it over, over and done with. He hurried them on but allowed Brother Edmund to stay close to John. Suddenly John stopped. He stood quite still, staring into space.

'What – what will they do with me when . . .'

Brother Edmund turned to face him and took his hands. 'I will take your body, Peg, and lay it to rest.'

'Not at a crossroads, out there in the open? Not like a felon – where they will stamp all over me, spit on me and . . .'

'Nay. I promise you. I will find a way. You will be laid in hallowed ground, like your father, like your friend Hugh.'

'With the lepers?'

'Perhaps.'

John nodded. 'All us crooked things together,' he said with a glance down at his foot, and they stumbled on.

The wind grew stronger, whipping the branches in their faces as they came out of the spindly trees. John remembered the little ship he had carved, tossing about on the trunk of the great beech tree in the avenue over towards Highwold. He thought of Will quiet in the churchyard there. And he thought of his angel still on the *Esperance*.

'I would have liked my angel with me,' he said in a small voice.

'Your angel?'

'I was carving it in stone, like my father did.'

'Where is it?'

'The Master has it.'

'I will find it and put it with you,' said Brother Edmund.

Again John nodded. He looked up. A little way ahead, half a dozen men waited for them on the path. Outlined against the waning moon, one of them held in his hand the unmistakeable shape of a noose swinging to and fro in the wind. The hangman. John shivered, drew closer to Brother Edmund and looked up at him. The grey eyes did not falter and a gentle hand on his shoulder seemed to give him the strength to go on. With few words, the two parties met and, beginning to struggle against the strengthening wind, pushed onwards towards the low hill where the gallows waited.

Dawn began to edge into the sky, turning the landscape grey and bleak. A prisoner's last moment must come as the sun broke the horizon. This morning, the great grey clouds massing over the sea hid the first rays, but the first faint angry light would be enough. The wind shrieked through the trees behind them and in the distance a single bell began to toll.

'For me?' thought John. But it would be for a

Morrow Mass at some church in Highwold, for the living to go and pray. Not for him. Too late for him. He felt his limbs begin to weaken and he reached out towards Brother Edmund. The tall monk took one of his hands in his and John held on to it, feeling like a little child, remembering his father's hand long, long ago.

Suddenly, ahead of them, there was a shout.

'Dear Christ Jesu in heaven – what has happened?'

The group of men who had met them surged forward. John peered upwards against the murk of the threatening sky. Where was the gibbet? He felt Brother Edmund beside him begin almost to run, his robe swirling as a sudden gust took it. John let go his hand but kept pace with him, limping against the force of a wind that was fast reaching gale strength.

At the top of the hill the men stood looking about them, bewildered. The gibbet lay in pieces scattered over the hilltop. For a moment, the men were speechless, staring about them at the broken timbers and the shallow pit where the main upright post had been rooted in. The upright lay beside the hole, clods of earth still sticking to the base. The crossbeam lay further away, split into two where the groove to take the noose had been. Nearby was a short metal bar and a sharp stone that had been used to batter the gibbet to the ground, shards of wood still sticking to them.

The hangman stared about him, his mouth agape. A sudden gust of wind set slivers of wood spinning away, whipping the noose from his limp fingers and tumbling it over the short, rough grass towards the edge of the hill. Another man, straw-haired, younger and faster, ran after it. Fumbling, he managed to scramble it up, dropping it and catching it, tripping and stumbling as he went, like the game of chasing the greasy pig at a fair. He threw it at the hangman's feet as though it were on fire. The other men began to panic, crossing themselves and backing away, tripping over each other and over the wreckage, the wind whirling at their hair, their clothes, into their very minds.

' 'Tis a miracle . . .'

' 'Tis Saint Nicholas lookin' after 'is own,' said the straw-haired man, looking at John. ' 'E's only a lad.'

'Nay, 'tis the work of – of the devil.'

'Aye, 'tis Old Nick 'imself.'

'The devil – aye, it's the devil.'

Two of the guards let out a terrified cry and raced off back the way they had come, yelling and hollering about the devil's work, and another flung himself to the ground, covering his head with his arms, whimpering. The hangman pulled himself together, grabbed up the noose and gave the man grovelling at his feet a swift kick.

'We must get 'im back to the jail till we can mend the gallows and do the job proper.'

'Nay,' said the straw-haired man. 'You can't 'ang 'im now. If once you fail, 'e must be set free.'

'*We* 'aven't failed . . . 'Twasn't us . . .'

'Don't matter. 'Tis the law.' The straw-haired man started to wrestle the noose from the hangman.

'Keep your wrists together and don't look at me,' said Brother Edmund in a low voice. Placing John in front of him, and keeping his own head up as if listening to the argument, surreptitiously Brother Edmund untied the rope around John's wrists, throwing it behind him down the side of the hill that led towards Fairholm. 'The man's right,' he muttered, 'they cannot hang you now.'

He waited a moment, quite still. Then, leaning towards John, still apparently engrossed in the dispute, he said, 'Peg, when I tell you, run. Go to the hospital. The brothers will take care of you and get you to the *Esperance*. No one will dare go in among the lepers to seek you. Keep out of sight as much as you can. I will try and divert them.'

He nodded towards the men still wrangling among the wreckage of the gibbet, almost coming to blows. Brother Edmund eased John behind him.

'Quietly down the hill, then run,' he said, over his shoulder, without turning his head. 'God go with you. Go now!' He strode forward towards the little crowd on the hilltop. As he went, John heard him say under his breath, 'And Jesu, Lord, forgive the lie I am about to tell.'

John dropped down below the lip of the hill, froze and listened. 'The boy has run,' he heard Brother Edmund say in a breathless voice, as if he had been in a struggle. 'I could hold him no longer. He went that way : . .'

'To Highwold . . .?' shouted the hangman. 'You let 'im go? Fool! Now we're in trouble.'

Furious voices turned on Brother Edmund, but, 'If we go now we may catch him,' he called, overtopping them. 'That way, I said . . .'

The men stampeded towards the far side of the hill. Quickly and without a sound, John slid down the hillside and waited in a clump of bushes at the bottom, trying to steady himself, to stop himself shaking. He took a few deep breaths and rubbed his wrists, still sore from the rope. He must keep his mind on escape, not what he had escaped from and what might still happen to him yet.

The noise of pounding feet faded. He began to snake through the bushes. He must make first for the river, then to Fairholm and the brothers. In full daylight now, the gale was howling across the open grassland, hurling before it loose branches and leaves, anything not fastened down. As John broke from the trees on to open ground a squall of freezing rain almost took his breath away. Keep out of sight, Brother Edmund had said, but where to hide? He staggered on towards the river, keeping low, beating into the wind and rain till he was soaked through and retching for breath.

Once across the river on the Fairholm side, he would be safer. Highwold men would think twice about venturing across. At last, there was the riverbank. He half-stumbled, half-rolled down it, praying that he had come out close to the ford. Cautiously scrambling back and raising his head, he squinted back over the bank to make sure no one was following. The rain was a grey sheet of mist over the countryside, but as far as he could see, nothing seemed to be moving.

He slithered back down to the water's edge. It looked shallow enough where he was and, almost from habit, he peeled off his sodden hose, hugged them and his clogs up to his chest and waded in. He swished across up to his knees and sat down on the far bank to wring out the hose, but they were still so wet he hung them round his neck, ready to start on for Fairholm. But now he was this far without mishap, before finding safety with the brothers, he would find Christina and send her home. She would surely realize he couldn't stay with her now.

He threw his clogs up the bank ahead of him, then slipping and sliding, mud everywhere, he climbed the bank on the Fairholm side. Hanging on to a tough clump of weed, he paused to gather the little strength he had left to haul himself up and go on.

Suddenly a twig snapped. His head went up as a brawny hand clapped down on his shoulder, grabbed his tunic and hauled him upwards, his feet pawing at the wet ground like a rag doll dragged by a baby.

'I'll teach ye to throw yer clogs at me, ye young devil,' said a gruff voice. 'I'll tan yer arse for yer, I will,' and he was slung up into the air, over a huge shoulder and carried along hell for leather into the wind.

Chapter 16

'Jack! Jack, put me down.'

'Stow yer garbage, lad. 'Tis quicker this way.'

Hairy Jack lumbered on over the wet grass, narrowly missing John's head as he swung through the trees, jolting him in the stomach till he was nearly sick.

'Jack! Please! Put – put me – put me . . .'

John started to choke and wheeze. The big sailor found a big tree for shelter and slid him down from his shoulder and on to the ground, giving his back an almighty thump as he landed. John's legs gave way. He subsided slowly into the sludge and, leaning forward on to his arms, started to laugh. Suddenly, he threw back his head and, rocking from side to side, his laughter grew wilder and wilder. Looking anxious, Jack pulled him upright and shook him hard and the laughter suddenly turned to great racking sobs that shook his whole body.

'There, lad, you're safe. I got you,' said Jack, and he wrapped him in a bear hug, lifting him clear of the ground, his scratched, muddy legs dangling in the air. Gently, Jack put him down again and ruffled the hair clinging to his head like sodden cords.

'You're safe now, lad,' he said again.

John gradually began to calm down, smearing his eyes and his nose with his hands and with the hose hanging round his neck. 'Where's my clogs?' he managed to say between hiccups.

'That all ye want?' said Jack, digging out the clogs from somewhere among his wet clothes. He dropped them and John shoved his bare feet into them, wriggling his toes.

'No, that isn't all,' said John. 'How did you . . .?'

'That Sir Richard – 'e told me. I went to the church to get you to go back to the ship, but you'd gone. I 'oped you'd gone to the Greyfriars. 'E were there with the brothers, lookin' right worried. Said Sir Basil, or some such name, 'ad made sure 'e were kept in the 'ospital. 'E were afeared they'd 'ang ye.'

'They nearly did.'

'I'd never 'ave let 'em,' said Jack. 'I'd 'ave got to you in time.'

John looked up with an uncertain little grin. 'It would have been a close thing,' he said, 'and there were a lot of them. Brother Edmund was with me.'

'They said 'e'd gone to see ye – to stay with ye afore . . .'

John nodded. 'He did. And now you've come. And now – now I'm . . .' He looked as if the sobbing might start again.

Jack took his arm. 'Enough o' this,' he said. 'Best get ye back to the ship.'

John looked up quickly. 'I must go to the mill first,' he said. 'I must.'

'To the mill? What for?'

'There's – there's someone there I've got to see. Someone – someone waiting for me there.'

A faint rumble of thunder made Jack peer out from under the tree and squint up at the still-gathering clouds.

'Nay, lad, we must go straight. Master's waitin'. We got to sail, quick. Them at Highwold won't expect us to leave in this weather, so we can sneak out with the tide an' ride out the storm out there.' He jerked his head towards the open sea just visible between the stunted trees. White waves reared and raced towards the shore.

'Is the ship mended then?'

'She'll do. The rest can wait till we get across to Flanders.'

'Why? Why not do it here?'

Jack looked down at him.

'There's trouble. The man they said you killed owned the *Elephant* and she were a Highwold ship.'

John's eyes widened. Everything was far more complicated than he had thought and it explained more of Sir Basil's fury. But he must see if Christina was in the mill. He must.

'They wouldn't try and take *Esperance* while she's this side, 'tis true. Too many Fairholm men to protect her. But on the way out . . . she'd be easy meat.'

'They'd sink her?'

Jack shrugged. 'Or take 'er for a prize. Retribution like. They'd 'ang the Master, whatever.' He glanced down at John again. 'They won't let you go again in a 'urry, neither.'

John shivered, his wet clothes sticking to him. Thunder growled in the distance over the sea. Jack crossed himself. 'Saint Nicholas an' all the saints watch over us,' he muttered and grabbed John's arm again. 'Come on, Peg. Master knows I've gone to find ye, but ship won't wait.'

A flash of lightning fizzed, lighting up the bleak wind-tossed landscape. Thunder rolled again, nearer this time. They ducked out from under the tree and with Jack half dragging him, John tried to keep up with the big sailor. Twice his foot gave way and he fell. The rain streamed down, seeming to try and hammer him into the earth. Each time, Jack hauled him up and on they went, the lightning and thunder moving in closer and the wind getting stronger and stronger as the eye of the storm whirled towards them. They could hear huge waves now, pounding the base of the cliff in the distance. As they breasted a rise, staggering against the wind, they saw the ragged arms of the mill, stark and clear, outlined against the sky, glittering spume flying up around it from the rocks far below.

'Couldn't we . . . ?'

Jack shook his head. 'Nay, Peg. She won't be there.'

'How do you know . . . ?'

'Sir Richard told me why she'd run off. 'E guessed she'd come lookin' for you, when she disappeared. 'E went to find 'er same time I came out after you. I reckon she'll be back at Eastwych by now.'

'Did he find her? Did he tell her what happened to me?'

'I never seen 'im, but – sure to. Nay, Peg, she won't

still be there. She'll 'ave gone back 'ome. Come on, will ye . . .'

Reluctantly, John gave a last look at the mill and they turned towards Fairholm, the wind behind them, hurling them forwards. The monastery lay ahead and, beyond, the remains of the town itself. Suddenly, a brilliant zigzag of lightning stabbed the sky. An almost simultaneous crash of thunder seemed to rip through John's head and send him reeling. Seconds later, there was an ominous rumbling and the earth shook. They stopped and looked back.

For a moment everything was still. Slowly, then faster, faster, the cliff seemed to split apart like a great animal opening its jaws. The mill hung on the edge, leaning, leaning, till with an immense shudder and a terrible rending scream of splitting timber, it keeled over and vanished over the edge, its sails offered up like arms raised towards heaven as it fell. Nothing remained but a cloud of boulders, clods of earth, flying rags and splinters.

John didn't move. Dust and gravel rained round them. He took a step towards the cleft reaching out along the hilltop but Jack had his arm. He looked up aghast at the big sailor.

'She – she might be there.'

Slowly, Jack shook his head.

'Nay, Peg. An' if she was . . . poor soul, she'll be gone now. Come on, lad, you can't do nothin'.'

Slowly, unwillingly, John allowed himself to be steered away from the cliff fall towards the monastery. As they went, a lone figure wrapped in a cloak pushed towards them, head down, against the wind.

'Sir Richard!' John began to run and the wind almost threw them together. But the man's face was white and anxious and he hardly looked at John.

'Where was she?' he said. 'Did she go home as I told her? I took her part of the way but – please God she didn't return.'

John looked back at Jack close behind him. Jack shook his head again, more positively this time.

'Nay, nay, sir. Surely not if you took 'er part way. And anyway, she wouldn't 'ave lasted through that,' and he jerked a thumb back towards the cliffs. 'Sir, we can't wait. We got to get to the ship.'

'She has already sailed,' said Sir Richard. 'See . . .'

They turned into the gale, peering along the coast through the trees. Branches lashed against each other in fury. Tossed like the little carved boat on the beech tree, the *Esperance* was fighting waves almost twice as high as herself. She nearly disappeared as they broke over her, but she stayed afloat and was clear of the river-mouth and heading out to sea.

' 'Tis too soon. She'll be done for out there,' said Jack, terror in his voice. ' 'Tis a lee shore.'

'It was that or die here,' shouted Sir Richard, against the wind. He pulled his cloak closer round him. 'The Master preferred the chance. He will anchor as soon as he can and ride out the storm.' A sudden gust tumbled him off balance and Jack grabbed him as he tottered backwards.

'Go quickly. No one will follow in this. Not yet. Get out to her before the storm abates, otherwise he will be forced to sail without you.'

'Take out a small boat in that?' Jack shook his head

towards the boiling surf. ' 'Sides, we'd 'ave to get to the quayside and pull downriver first. They'd never let us get away.'

'Then we must hide the boy. Here,' said Richard, looking down at John for the first time, 'take this. You are soaked through and shivering.'

He took off his cloak and wrapped it round John. But John was still looking back towards the place where the mill had been. Jack followed his gaze.

'I'm thinkin',' he said, his hand on John's shoulder, tucking the cloak round him. 'We left a boat from the *Esperance* down on the beach where we was shovellin' away the sand. That would be nearer, if 'tis still there. They . . .' and he jerked his head towards the river and Highwold on the far bank, 'they couldn't see us from down there. But launchin' it in this . . .'

'Let's try,' said Sir Richard. 'How will we get down?'

'There's a path,' said Jack, leading the way.

'It's near the mill,' said John, his face brightening. Perhaps they would be able to see if anyone had been inside. At least he would know, one way or the other. He hurried after Jack and the wind bellied out the cloak till he nearly took off like a ship setting sail.

'Thank you, Sir Richard,' he said, 'but I'll manage better without it,' and he handed the cloak back to the spindly figure battling with the wind beside him. Suddenly, Sir Richard looked behind him.

'Hurry, Jack,' he said anxiously to the big sailor. 'Get yourself and the boy out of sight.'

John looked round. In the distance a party of horsemen were pounding through the storm across the open grassland towards the monastery.

Jack paused in mid-stride. 'The girl's father?' he said. Sir Richard nodded. Jack began to run John towards the pathway down the cliff.

'I'll go back and hold them off as long as I can. God be with you.' The wind took Sir Richard's voice and hurled it into the distance but Jack raised an arm to say he had heard. Sir Richard turned, threw his cloak over his shoulders and hurried away, blown towards the monastery silhouetted against the storm clouds.

The path down to the beach was buried in rubble. Stumbling, constantly glancing back towards the monastery, they searched about for another way down.

'Reckon we could get down 'ere,' said Jack, jabbing a finger over the edge. 'Means a climb but I think 'tis safe enough.'

Gingerly, he put a foot over the cliff edge on to a boulder, the top of a colossal heap the storm had wedged against the cliff, making a kind of giant stair downwards. John followed him and together they slipped and scrambled, sometimes falling, scraping their legs and arms and almost rolling the last few feet to the bottom.

'You all right, Peg?' said Jack, getting to his feet. He looked along the beach towards a small boat pulled up close to the base of the cliff. 'Look, she's yonder. Come on.'

John sat up on the shingle. The wreck of the mill was only a short distance away, scattered over sand and pebbles and rock pools. He struggled up, his foot giving way and almost throwing him back down again. As he raised his head, he gasped.

She was there. Christina lay on the rain-blackened rocks, her arms spread wide as if she had flown down on the wind from the clifftop like a seabird. John watched, holding his breath. Did she move or was it just the swell of the shallow water beneath her? Without taking his eyes from her, he heaved himself to his feet and hobbled over the soft sand and boulders towards her. She didn't move.

In the rock pool in which she lay, dark weeds surrounded her shorn head. The fronds rippled backwards and forwards, backwards and forwards, looking for all the world like the long, thick hair she had cut off so bravely. He stood looking down at her still, pale face, then dropped to his knees beside her and took her cold hand in his. Her eyes fluttered then were gone.

'Christina,' he said, 'Christina, please don't . . . It's Peg. I'm here. I never left you. They took me – I tried, I tried to . . .'

Slowly her eyes opened, but he knew she could see nothing.

'Peg,' she murmured. 'I – I wished very – hard for you to come and – and you did.'

He nodded, dropping his head to her hand, unable to speak.

'They can't marry me to anyone now, Peg,' she said. 'I'm safe. Safe.' She smiled, her eyes wide open, staring at something he couldn't see, and for a moment, he was dazzled.

'Peg . . . I didn't want them to . . . they – they

didn't . . .' He leant closer but she sighed and said no more. Her eyes misted over, and with no more than a soft, shuddering breath, she was gone. He knelt beside her in the rock pool, his heart tangled and heavy like the weeds. He couldn't move.

From behind him, Jack gently reached over, released his fingers from her hand and pulled him away. He huddled on the shingle, his eyes still upon her. Jack closed Christina's eyes, crossed her arms on her breast and said in a quiet voice. 'Come on, lad, there's nothing you can do for the little lass now.' He jerked his head upwards towards the monastery on the cliff. 'They'll take care of 'er. 'Er father must 'ave come lookin' for 'er. Sir Richard will know where to look. They'll find 'er and lay 'er to rest.'

He lifted John to his feet and turned him away. Tears blinding him, John almost stumbled over something lying on the shingle. Christina's saddle bag lay open, its contents spilled across the pebbles. He brushed his arm across his eyes and stooped down.

'What's this?'

Among the mouldering food lay a piece of splintered black wood with a groove cut in it. Close by lay a dagger, sharp as a scream, blood covering the blade and the handle. John looked back at the still figure, the weed waving softly round her head. Could it be true? Is that what she had meant? 'They didn't hang you . . .' He looked up, his face hot, his breath coming quickly as realization flooded through him.

She had done it. Christina had killed Lord Lovat.

And Christina had destroyed the gallows so he would not die instead of her.

He picked up the dagger and the fragment of wood to take with him and looked down at them for a moment. Could she really have done it? On her own? He looked back at her and remembered her climbing down the side of the house, tearing across the countryside astride her horse, standing up to her father. He smiled. Yes. She could have done anything she chose.

Suddenly, he changed his mind. He went back to the silent body and carefully placed the dagger and the fragment of wood between her hands. Sir Basil would find them and know what she had done. He might even try to understand why.

With a brief smile and a nod, John turned and, biting hard on his lips, crossed the beach to Jack, already tugging the small boat towards the waves. They were diminishing now as the wind veered and lessened and the storm passed overhead. No time to lose. Together they launched her, waded out and scrambled in. Jack took both the oars, but John squeezed in beside him, shifted him over on the cross bench and took an oar from him.

'You, lad? You ain't no seaman. Carvin's more your line.'

'Stow yer garbage, Jack,' said John with a grin. 'I can do anything.'

Together they started to pull for the *Esperance*, riding at anchor out at sea.

A note from the author

Long, long ago, the village of Dunwich on the east coast of England was a thriving seaport. It was the second largest town in England after London. At about the time of *Ship's Angel*, the harbour mouth was silted up and the town lost its trade. Over the years, cliff falls have tipped many of the remaining buildings into the sea, including a church. All that is left is a small, ancient village, part of the monastery and a new church.

Not far from Dunwich, near a village called Wantesdon, you can find an avenue of huge, old beech trees. They are called the Quincunx trees. On them, Victorian seamen carved little ships to commemorate sailors who had died, especially at sea. The tradition is an old one, and may date from time immemorial.

In the late thirteenth century, a young girl called Christina, daughter of Roger of Honeford, was mentioned in the town records. She was guilty of 'destroying the town gibbet'. Why she did it and what happened to her is not known.

* * *

The story of *Ship's Angel* is based loosely on all these events, but the towns of Fairholm, Eastwych and Highwold are imaginary, as are Christina's reasons for her actions. However, if you ever visit Dunwich, go into the museum. You will find many maps, models, pictures and other legends of the 'town that disappeared into the sea'.